DEAD IS SO LAST YEAR

marlene perez

G RAPHIA

HOUGHTON MIFFLIN HARCOURT

Boston New York 2009

Requests for permission to make copies of any part of the work should be
submitted online at www.harcourt.com/contact or mailed to the following address:
Permissions Department, Houghton Mifflin Harcourt Publishing Company,
6277 Sea Harbor Drive, Orlando, Florida 32887-6777.

Graphia and the Graphia logo are registered trademarks of
Houghton Mifflin Harcourt Publishing Company.

www.graphiabooks.com

The text of this book is set in Adobe Jenson.

Library of Congress Cataloging-in-Publication Data
Perez, Marlene.
Dead is so last year / by Marlene Perez.
p. cm.
Summary: In the beach town of Nightshade, California, home to both human and
supernatural beings, the Giordano sisters find summer employment and uncover mysteries
involving doppelgangers and oversized football players.
ISBN 978-0-15-206216-3 (pbk.)
[1. Supernatural—Fiction. 2. Psychic ability—Fiction. 3. Sisters—Fiction.] I. Title.
PZ7.P4258De 2009
[Fic]—dc22
2008048426

ISBN 978-0-15-206216-3

Printed in the United States of America
QUM 10 9 8 7 6 5 4 3

To my sister Teresa,
who I can always laugh with

DEAD IS SO LAST YEAR

CHAPTER ONE

"*Daisy, you're back!*" Chief Mendez said when he answered the front door. "How was Italy?"

"It was amazing," I said. My mom had taken all of the Giordano women—which means my sisters, Rose and Poppy, and our Grandma Giordano—on a surprise vacation to Italy, as soon as school let out.

I think part of the reason for the trip had been that Poppy, who'd recently had a rather unusual breakup, had been moping around graveyards instead of celebrating her recent graduation from Nightshade High. I supposed that's just the way things went when your first serious boyfriend was a ghost.

"Ryan's not here," the chief continued.

"He's not?" I said, disappointed. I hadn't seen my boyfriend in three weeks, and as glorious as the trip had been, I was glad to be back home in Nightshade.

"He's at football practice," Ryan's dad continued. "Why don't you head on over there and surprise him? He didn't think you were coming back until tomorrow."

"We took an earlier flight and got back late last night," I said. "But football started already? So early?"

"Summer conditioning," his dad explained. "Coach Wullf is pushing to get us into the division playoffs this year."

"Uh, that's great," I said. I didn't know much about football, even though I'd very briefly been a cheerleader during football season last year.

"Tell your mom I'll call her about this case I'm working on," he said. "And Daisy, Nightshade wasn't the same without the Giordanos around."

Chief Mendez and my mom worked together to solve crimes. She was a psychic investigator. For a long time, I had thought that only Rose and Poppy had inherited Mom's psychic gifts, but I'd recently discovered that I was psychic, too.

"Mom's still in Italy," I explained. "She got caught up in a case over there. We flew home with Grandma Giordano."

"I'll have to manage without her, then," he replied. "Call the station if you need anything. I worry about you girls there alone."

"Grandma Giordano is going to check up on us," I explained. "And she may even stay over occasionally if Mom has to be away much longer."

"That's reassuring," Ryan's dad replied. "Tell your grandmother I said hello."

I wondered how they knew each other. Grandma spent most of her time at her condo in a 55-and-over community nearby. That is, when she wasn't volunteering for a myriad of charity functions. But Nightshade was a small town. Everyone knew everyone, at least to say hello.

"See you later." I'd managed to bribe Poppy into letting me have the car, so I decided to head to the school to track down Ryan. When I pulled up, a group of players were running drills on the football field. Even from as far away as I was, I could hear grunts and groans as the coaches yelled at them.

A cluster of girls sat under an easy-up tarp, sheltered from the hot sun. As I passed them, I saw it was a group of cheer-leaders. There was a huge container of Gatorade for the players, while the girls were drinking iced tea or lemonade.

My friend Samantha Devereaux bounded over. "Daisy, you're back! How was Italy?"

"It was great," I said. "I'll tell you all about it later."

I felt a thrill when I spotted Ryan. He was hard to pick out of the crowd, since they all wore practice jerseys and helmets, but I recognized his tall frame.

I gave him an enthusiastic wave. A few minutes later, a pair of muscular arms encircled my waist and lifted me off the ground.

"You're finally back," Ryan's voice said. "I missed you so much," he added in a lower tone.

As he set me down, I realized that the Ryan I'd left a few short weeks ago had changed. I looked him up and down in shock. He was now a rippling mass of muscle.

I'd been gone only three weeks and Ryan looked twenty pounds heavier and about three inches taller. He was gorgeous. I loved the way the tan emphasized his green eyes, and the curls at the nape of his neck—were gone! He'd shaved his head.

"Ryan?" I said. "You look . . . different." He'd always been tall, but now he towered over me.

He ran a hand over his hair. "It was just too hot. All the guys have been shaving their heads."

"You've gained a lot of muscle, too."

"Yeah, Sean and I have been hitting the weights really hard. Coach wants us to be in shape by the time the season starts."

Sean was Samantha's boyfriend and my next-door neighbor. He was also Ryan's best friend.

A whistle blew and one of the coaches said, "Break's over, boys."

Ryan grabbed a cup of Gatorade and chugged it before he said, "Gotta get back to it. How about we meet at Slim's in an hour? We've got a lot to talk about."

I nodded, and watched him run back to the field. My brain was still processing my boyfriend's physical transformation. Werewolf or not, he'd really packed on the muscle while I'd been gone.

"So, any particular reason why you have that glassy-eyed stare?" Samantha asked.

"Ryan," I confessed. "I can't believe how . . ."

"Hot he looks," Sam finished my sentence. "Yeah, you came

back in the nick of time." She glanced back at the rest of the cheerleaders, then whispered, "Penny Edwards was all over Ryan while you were gone. She's done everything but tie herself up in a red ribbon, not that he was interested."

I shrugged. Ryan and I were on solid ground. If Elise Wilder hadn't tempted him, I wasn't worried about Penny Edwards. Elise was a gorgeous girl who'd moved back to Nightshade a few months back. She and Bane Paxton were now a pretty steady item, but she still made me nervous. Maybe it was her claws.

"I'm heading to Slim's to wait for Ryan," I said. "Want to come along?"

Samantha glanced over at the rest of the cheerleaders. "Sure," she said. "Cheerleading practice is over, anyway." She grabbed her purse and then said, "Can I catch a ride with you? My car is in the shop."

"Of course you can ride with me, but is everything okay?" I said as we headed for the car I shared with Rose and Poppy.

"Don't look at me like that, Daisy," she said. "It really *is* in the shop. The worst of the Devereaux troubles are finally over."

Samantha's mom and dad were getting a divorce and they'd lost most of their money, which meant they had to sell their huge house. The Devereauxs had downsized and Sam had moved into a small townhouse near the UC Nightshade campus with her father.

"How are things with your dad?" I asked. Samantha's dad had been a colleague of my dad's before he disappeared six years ago. Some people in town thought that my father hadn't disappeared at all. Supposedly, he'd run away with another woman, but my mom refused to believe those rumors.

"Surprisingly good," she said. "And I got a job. And they're willing to work around my cheerleading schedule when school starts."

"A job? That's great, Sam. Where?"

"That cute boutique. Tete de Mort."

Designer goth and nothing in the store was less than two hundred dollars. Was Sam reverting to her fall look?

"Don't worry," she said, reading my mind. "No more dressing up like a vampire. Not now that I know they really do exist. Dead is so last year."

"A job is a great idea," I said.

"It's only part-time, but I get a thirty percent discount," she replied. "Want me to see if they need any more help?"

A summer job? My oldest sister, Rose, was working at the college, at a research lab. Maybe I could find something, too. I could use the extra money and I was getting tired of asking Mom for cash all the time. Besides, I had my eye on this very expensive gourmet-cooking class.

It seemed serendipitous when we pulled up in front of Slim's Diner and I saw the Help Wanted sign in the window.

Slim's was a fifties-style diner, complete with red leather booths, lots of stainless steel, and a permanent smell of grease. It was also the place to get the best hamburger in town.

When we walked in, the jukebox immediately stopped playing. I held my breath, waiting for some message conveyed through song, but it didn't start again.

"Is it broken?" I asked Flo. Flo was my favorite waitress at Slim's. Despite her name and occupation, she was the antithesis of a fifties-diner waitress. No pink uniform and beehive for Flo. She was in her midtwenties, buff, with serious tats, and she always wore T-shirts and jeans to work. Today's shirt read VOICES TELL ME THINGS. EVIL THINGS.

"The jukebox is pouting," she replied, from her perch at a counter barstool. "Been cranky since you've been gone."

Slim's was nearly empty, so we managed to grab my favorite booth in front of the big window. When Flo came over to take our order, I pointed to the sign. "You need help, Flo? I'm looking for a summer job."

She shrugged. "Guess so. Slim must have put that up. Come back in the morning at five and talk to him."

Wait. Five A.M.?

"There's really a Slim? I had no idea. Why haven't I ever seen him? I thought he was made up, like Mrs. Butterworth or Colonel Sanders," Samantha said.

"Uh, Sam, I'm pretty sure there really was a Colonel Sanders," I pointed out.

"Oh, you know what I mean."

We ordered large chocolate shakes and fries.

"Now tell me all about Italy," Sam said.

We talked about my vacation, but I left out a few of the scarier bits, like the part where I'd been chased by banshees. Thanks to my psychic powers and a little espresso, I'd managed to fight them off. There was enough supernatural stuff going on in Nightshade, so there was no need to import it. Plenty of the strange in Nightshade.

Sean and Ryan entered the restaurant as Flo was delivering our order. I took a closer look at Sean and noticed that he'd bulked up almost as much as Ryan had.

"Perfect timing," Sean said. He snagged a french fry from the plate. Sam smacked his hand.

"Get your own," she said. Then she smiled at him. "Okay, we'll share, but it'll cost you a bite of your burger."

Ryan said, "Hi, Flo, can I get a burger and fries? Burger extra, extra rare."

"And I'll take a side of E. coli to go with that," I said. "What's with the still-moving meat?" But I knew the answer to my own question. He was a wolf boy. Of course he craved raw meat sometimes.

Ryan shrugged. "Coach says it'll help us with our game."

"I've been craving raw steak all day," Sean said.

Samantha and I both shuddered.

Ryan just grinned at me. Suddenly, I felt shy, like my boyfriend was a different person. Weird, especially since we'd been friends even before we were boyfriend and girlfriend. Ryan had always been one of the hottest guys in school, but he had gone supernova since I'd left for vacation.

While the guys waited for their food, I decided to feed the jukebox and maybe coax it into playing again. The jukebox at Slim's, which I'd nicknamed Lil, had a mind of its own. It played what it wanted to when it wanted to.

Ryan came with me.

"I missed you," he said.

"I missed you, too. Did you get my postcard?" I pretended to study the jukebox selection intently, even though I knew the playlist by heart. How dorky was I? Shy with my own boyfriend?

I chose "Fade Into You" by Mazzy Star, which was a song Ryan and I had danced to at prom. The jukebox started, but the song wasn't something I'd chosen. Instead, "Go Away" by Elvis Costello came on. Just business as usual at Slim's. Sometimes Lil dropped hints about whatever was going on in my life. But today, she just sounded mad.

"You look—good," I said.

Ryan smiled. "I'm the same old me," he said. "Except now you know I'm a werewolf."

"What about Sean?"

"He doesn't know I'm a Were," Ryan said.

"Are you going to tell him?" I asked.

Ryan thought about it. "I don't think it's a big deal, but I'll tell him." I was glad to see his attitude had changed. Not that long ago, he'd been trying to keep it a secret from me.

"Good, but what I really meant is what's going on with him? His neck is as big as my thigh. Is he a shifter, too?"

"No. I told you, he's just been working out."

Three weeks of working out and Sean already looked like that? Only in Nightshade. I decided to put it in the back of my mind for now and concentrate on letting my boyfriend know how much I'd missed him.

CHAPTER TWO

When I got home from the diner, I was in a great mood. Poppy, however, was not. She was sitting in the living room, with the shades drawn. Her laptop was on the table beside her, and the screen revealed our vacation pictures, which she'd obviously uploaded from the digital camera.

"The Trevi Fountain was so beautiful," she said, then sighed. "I wish we were still in Italy."

"Funny," I said, "because you looked miserable the entire time we were there."

"Well, it's even harder being back in Nightshade," Poppy said. "Everything reminds me of Gage."

Poppy's ghost boyfriend had haunted Nightshade just long enough to take Poppy to the prom before he finally left this world forever, breaking her heart in the process.

"Have you been out of the house at all today?" I asked. I looked toward the window and, after concentrating for a moment, used my telekinesis to pull open the curtains and let in some sunshine. "It's a beautiful day."

"Of course I've been out," Poppy said indignantly.

"Going to the graveyard doesn't count."

Poppy crossed her arms and gave me a pouty look. My social-butterfly sister hadn't been the same since her heart was broken.

"Gage is gone, Poppy," I said gently. "He wouldn't want you to—"

"How do you know what he wanted?" she snapped, then looked contrite. "I'm sorry, Daisy, I know you're trying to help. It's just that I miss him so much." Tears filled her eyes.

It killed me to see my sister so sad, but Poppy had been moping far too long. Her hair looked like it hadn't been washed in days, and her skin was pale. Her jeans were starting to hang on her and I wondered how she'd lost weight when we ate all that pasta in Italy. Actually, come to think of it, I ate the pasta; Poppy just picked at it.

I sat next to Poppy and put an arm around her delicate shoulders. "We've got a whole summer of fun ahead of us," I said. "We have the house to ourselves . . ."

"What else is new?" Poppy said. "Mom's usually always working when she is around, and Dad . . ."

"I know," I said. Our father had disappeared during a research trip, when I was twelve. Almost six years had passed and we still had no idea what had happened to him.

But a few months back, I had gotten a lead: It seemed he might be being held against his will by the Scourge, a covert group whose goal was to wipe out the paranormal population.

But my father was a norm, so what could they want with him? And if they did have him, where were they keeping him? These were all things I planned to find out this summer, and I had a feeling my mom did, too.

Finding my father was practically all she had thought about since he'd been gone. Even when there were whispers that Rafe Giordano had just abandoned his family, Mom had never lost hope that he was alive and well and eager to get back to us. I hoped she was right.

I snapped out of my momentary melancholy and got back to cheering up Poppy. "I have an idea," I said. "We should have a party!"

Poppy gave me a horrified look. "Are you kidding?" she said. "Mom would kill us if we had a party while she's away. And she'd find out about it somehow. You know how people in Nightshade talk."

There was a jangling of keys and the front door opened to admit our older sister, Rose, still clothed in the lab coat she wore to work. "Not to mention the fact that mom is psychic, geniuses," she said.

She must have overheard our conversation. Or, she could have just read our minds. Rose didn't like to eavesdrop on other people's thoughts for no reason, but her telepathy was really strong, so it sometimes happened by accident.

"I don't mean having a party here at the house," I said. "Let's have it at the beach."

The beach wasn't too far from our house, and it was Poppy's favorite place to hang out in the summertime. If that didn't get a reaction, nothing would.

"The beach?" She brightened for a minute, then deflated. "I don't have a bathing suit to wear."

"But you have tons of suits," Rose said. "Plus all my hand-me-downs."

Poppy's expression grew gloomier. "I'm tired of them all."

Do something, Rose's voice said in my mind. *I blew it.*

Okay, okay, I thought back. *We've got to convince her to have this party. What are her favorite things?*

Talking on the phone, Rose replied. *And shopping.*

That's it!

I glanced quickly at Poppy, but she didn't seem to notice that Rose and I were communicating nonverbally.

"We'll take you shopping for a new suit," I said rashly. Shopping wasn't my favorite pastime, but Poppy had always come through for me in a wardrobe emergency.

"Can we have a bonfire?" she asked.

"Does that mean you'll show?"

"I promise," she replied. "It will be good to spend some quality time with a bunch of our friends before everybody starts leaving for college." Like Rose, Poppy would be going to UC Nightshade, so she'd be staying in town.

"Then a bonfire and a picnic," I said. "And all our friends

will be there. It'll be fun." They'd be there if I had to drag every single one of them to the beach.

Poppy got up and hunted for the cordless phone, which used to be permanently attached to her ear. "I'll call Candy. How about Saturday? That's enough time to plan an amazing party." In a moment, Poppy had wandered into the kitchen and was happily chattering away on the phone to her best friend.

"A beach party is a good idea," Rose said. "I hope it gets her out of her funk."

"So do I," I said. "How was your day?"

Rose looked exhausted. "Long," she said, "but so interesting. I think I'm going to learn a lot from Dr. Franken this summer. She's a brilliant scientist. And she was friends with dad, you know."

I stiffened. "No, I didn't know that," I said. "What's her area of study?"

"Genetics," Rose said.

"You mean like DNA and cloning and stuff?"

"Well, she's not cloning anyone," Rose said. "That's a pretty sensitive issue. She was telling me that she and Dad had been collaborating before he—"

Rose was cut off when Poppy bounded back into the living room. "Mom's on the phone," she announced, then put the phone on speaker mode.

"Hi, Mom," we said in unison.

"Hi, girls," she said.

"How's Italy?" Rose asked.

"About the same as when you left here yesterday," Mom said. She chuckled as she said it. Her case must be going well.

I was glad she sounded happy. I was afraid she'd be lonely over there all by herself. But she was more worried about us, all alone in the house, even though we were old enough to take care of ourselves. After all, Rose was in college, Poppy had just graduated high school, and I'd be a senior at Nightshade High in the fall.

Before hanging up, she asked if one of us could mail a certain notebook to her. She needed it to compare some old notes to the case she was working on now.

"Ooh, the post office will be closed by the time I get out of the lab," Rose said.

"I'll take care of it," I said quickly. I wanted to prove to Mom how responsible we were.

"Thanks, Daisy," she said. "I knew I could count on you. Now, be careful, girls. Don't let any strangers in the house. I love you."

Poppy nearly jumped out of her skin when the doorbell rang right after we hung up with Mom. "Who could that be?"

Rose laughed. "It's probably just Nicholas." Nicholas Bone was Rose's boyfriend.

"Or Ryan," I said. "He's coming over to watch movies."

Poppy rolled her eyes as she went to answer the door. "You two and your werewolf boyfriends."

It turned out to be Nicholas. I could understand what Rose saw in him. He was handsome: tall, with pale skin, reddish-brown hair, and brandy-colored eyes. His hair was the exact shade of our Irish setter, Sparky, who died of old age last year. Nicholas also was, as Poppy had mentioned, a werewolf.

"Hi, Poppy," Nicholas said. "How are things going? Feeling any better?" Nicholas knew all about Poppy's unusual breakup; she had met Gage the ghost at Mort's Mortuary, which was the funeral home owned by Nicholas's father.

Poppy shrugged and stepped aside for Rose, who was rushing toward the door, obviously thrilled to be reunited with her boyfriend. Nicholas's eyes sparkled when he saw her. It didn't seem to matter to him that she was still in her lab coat looking slightly disheveled. He still loved her.

As Poppy and I snuck upstairs to give them some privacy, I couldn't help but wonder if Ryan loved me like that.

I didn't know why I was stressing, except that Ryan was only getting better looking as time passed, and he was no slouch to begin with. It made me conscious that I was still plain old Daisy, okay-looking but certainly nothing special. I didn't have Elise Wilder's dangerous beauty or even the softer glamour of the rest of my own family.

"Want me to do your makeup?" Poppy asked. "I may not have a date tonight, but that doesn't mean you shouldn't look stunning for yours."

I nodded, then followed Poppy into the bathroom, where

she rummaged around in her makeup bag until she found just the right shade of eye shadow. "This will make your eyes really pop," she said as she applied it. When Poppy was done working her magic, I had to admit I looked pretty great. I blinked at my reflection in the mirror. My blue eyes really stood out.

"I don't even look like myself," I said, fluttering my mascaraed lashes. "Now I look like someone people *expect* to see with Ryan."

"What are you talking about?" Poppy scoffed. "Daisy, you're beautiful even without makeup. And Ryan's crazy about you. You know that, right?"

"Right."

"So why would you say something like that?"

I shrugged. "You should see him, Poppy," I said. "He's even more gorgeous than when we left."

"So?"

"So, I'm just ordinary Daisy Giordano."

"Who he completely adores," Poppy responded. "And you are far from ordinary."

My head knew that my sister was right. Ryan could have dated any girl in school and he chose me. Now, if I could only start to believe the "far from ordinary" part. It wasn't easy having a boyfriend who put the *super* in *supernatural*.

CHAPTER THREE

When the alarm rang bright and early the next morning, I almost rolled over and hit the SNOOZE button. Jet lag was finally catching up with me, and I had stayed up too late watching movies with Ryan—well, mostly watching movies. But since I'd never seen the elusive Slim and I really did want a summer job, I forced my eyelids open and went downstairs to put on a pot of coffee. Coffee and good chocolate were the two things in life I found necessary to function properly.

After a quick shower, I threw on what I thought would be interview-appropriate clothing: navy cotton dress pants and a white shirt. I thought my usual summer flip-flops would be a little too casual, so I rooted through my closet until I found some closed-toe sandals. I braided my hair in a single plait and grabbed the keys. I didn't forget to bring along the notebook I had to send my mom, which I figured I'd mail after my interview.

It was still dark out when I left the house. Main Street looked deserted, but you could never tell what might be lurking in the shadows in Nightshade. The lights were on at Slim's and the Donut Hole, the new donut shop across the street. My mouth watered, but there was no time to grab a quick sugar fix. I needed to get to my interview.

I had my pick of parking spots, so I pulled into one right in front of Slim's. As I got out of the car, Mr. Krayson, my statistics teacher, exited the donut shop, stuffing donuts in his mouth as fast as he could.

"Hi, Mr. Krayson," I called out. He didn't answer, or even act like he heard me, but continued to chew. Little chunks of jelly donuts sprayed everywhere, but he didn't seem to notice. Gross.

I shrugged. He was always on a diet. Maybe he was embarrassed to be seen eating so many donuts.

The door to Slim's was locked so I tapped on the glass. It opened, seemingly of its own volition. I stepped into an empty restaurant. I'd been there a million times, but the utter silence spooked me a little. Flo had said Slim would be here at five, but there was no sign of him.

"Hello?" I said. "Is anybody here?" There was no reply.

This was the weirdest job interview I'd ever been on. Granted, I'd never had a job interview before, but I was pretty sure there was supposed to be another person involved.

I wandered into the back, getting a secret thrill from treading forbidden territory. I loved to cook, and Slim's spotless and orderly kitchen met with my full approval.

There was a row of shiny knives on the counter, along with

a cutting board. I stepped closer and examined the knives. They were Global knives, favorites with professional chefs. My hands itched to use them. I ran a finger along one of the blades. Honed to perfection.

"Hello?" I said again, but there was still no answer. Slim's was due to open any minute and it looked like Slim had left in the middle of preparation. I washed my hands and decided I'd make a pot of coffee while I waited. The enormous vat of a coffeemaker was in the front wait station. Coffee and filters were already in the machine, so all I had to do was press a button.

I snooped around some more and found a pan of cinnamon rolls proofing near the oven.

They need to go in the oven soon, or they'll overproof. I had picked up a stray thought—which sometimes happened even when I wasn't trying to read someone's mind—and then looked around. I wasn't alone, but I couldn't for the life of me figure out where the person could be hiding.

I checked the temperature and then slid them into the oven and set the timer.

That finished, I went to check the coffee. It was ready, so I poured myself a cup, added lots of cream and sugar, and went back to the kitchen.

Where was Slim? Was he hiding somewhere, watching my every move? It was spooking me out.

The specials are veggie omelets and banana pancakes. Another hint from my mysterious observer, wherever he was. By now, I was almost sure that it was Slim who was my silent watcher.

I could have chopped the veggies using my telepathic skills, especially since Poppy was always nagging me to practice, but I wanted to try out those knives. And besides, I had a sneaking suspicion a real cook might consider that cheating. A lot of people in Nightshade already knew I was psychic, but there was no need to advertise it. I'd do the work the old-fashioned way.

The knives chopped like a dream, but I was careful. I'd stop working intermittently, to look over my shoulder. I could still sense a presence. Besides, I didn't want to get blood all over that pristine kitchen.

When the vegetables were chopped, I washed my hands again, then started on the pancake batter. That finished, I wiped down the counters and cleaned all the utensils I'd used.

I'd done as much as I could when the timer for the cinnamon rolls rang off. I found a couple of oven mitts and took the rolls out of the oven. I almost dropped the whole tray when a masculine voice said, "You're hired."

I turned around, but there was nobody there.

"I'm sorry," I said. "Did somebody say something?"

"I said," the voice continued, "that you're hired. You're looking for a job, right?"

Still no sign of anyone else on the premises. "Are you a ghost?"

The voice sounded amused now. "Flo said you were an intelligent girl. I'm not a ghost."

"Invisible?" I guessed again.

"Very good," he said. Invisible hands clapped.

"I'm Daisy," I said. "And you are . . . ?"

"Slim," the man said. "Not my real name, of course. Just one of Florence's little jokes. Griffin is my given name, but you can call me Slim. Everyone does."

Florence? Flo's real name is Florence?

"My younger sister has a somewhat unusual sense of humor," the voice continued. "Florence will be in shortly, but in the meantime, I expect Officer Denton and his lovely fiancé will be wanting their breakfast. Be a dear and let them in."

Slim was Flo's brother? Nightshade really was full of secrets. Now that I thought about it, I didn't really know much about Flo, despite the fact that I'd been coming to Slim's for years.

"Was this some sort of test?" I said as I set the cinnamon rolls on the counter. I felt relieved that I didn't have to answer a bunch of questions. I had been geared up for the *What do you think are your greatest strengths?* question.

In reply, a ring of keys was tossed in the air. I caught it on reflex but then stood there, mouth agape, until Slim cleared his throat.

I went to the front of the restaurant and found Officer Denton and his fiancé at the door, just as Slim had said they'd be.

I unlocked the door and let them in. "Good morning, Daisy," Officer Denton said. "I didn't know you worked here."

"I didn't, either," I said, under my breath.

After I took their orders, I went to the kitchen, not sure what to do next.

"Uh, I need two orders of banana pancakes, with pecans," I said to the air.

"You'll find an order pad and some pens in that drawer," Slim said.

"Which drawer?"

"My apologies," Slim said. A second later, a knife floated into the air and then pointed in the general direction of the correct drawer.

I grabbed the pad and wrote out the order, then hung it on the little wheel thingie I'd seen Flo use a million times before.

Gradually, more people started to filter in. A couple of coffee drinkers at the counter I could handle, but when the booths started to fill up, I began to panic. But I didn't have time to worry as I ran around getting orange juice and coffee, taking orders, and generally losing my mind.

Where was Flo? About ten seconds from meltdown, she strolled in.

"Where have you been?" I panted.

"Sorry," she said. "I was . . . unavoidably detained. Did you work everything out with Slim?"

"Not exactly," I replied. "He just told me I was hired, and pointed me toward the customers."

"He must like you," she said.

"Flo, a little service here," called one of the regulars.

For the next hour and a half, I worked harder than I'd ever worked in my life. When the breakfast rush finally calmed down, I collapsed on a barstool at the counter.

"Why don't you take a break, Daisy?" Flo said. "Have a soda or cup of coffee. I can handle it for now."

"Thanks," I said. "I could use something to drink."

"Coffee's on the house," Flo said, as she waved my money away.

"I need to call my sisters," I said. "I told them I had an interview, but they're probably wondering where the heck I've been this whole time."

I called home, but when the machine picked up, I just left a message.

Then I took my caffeine and went to sit outside for a few minutes. My feet hurt and I could feel a blister forming on my heel. I hadn't planned on working in the shoes I'd worn to my interview.

I saw Miss McBennett, who worked at the post office and had to be nearly eighty. She was going into the donut shop. I waved, but she seemed to be in a hurry to get her donuts. Those donuts must be something—better than Krispy Kreme donuts, if that was even possible.

Seeing Miss McBennett reminded me that I had to mail that package to my mom, so I told Flo I'd be right back and walked around the corner to the post office. Sitting there behind the counter was none other than . . . Miss McBennett?

How could that be? I was sure that it was her I'd seen not five minutes before, going into the Donut Hole. I didn't think an eighty-year-old woman—not even my grandma, who walked three miles every day—could make it there and back that quickly.

"Daisy? Can I help you?" Miss McBennett asked, seeing me standing there with a confused look on my face. "Is something wrong?"

I collected myself. "Didn't I just see you at the donut shop?"

"Goodness, no," Miss McBennett said. "I didn't live this long by eating junk food. I've never been to that donut shop and I don't plan to go."

"Oh. I guess it must have been someone who just looked a lot like you," I said. After mailing the package, I wanted to stop at the Donut Hole and see if the Miss McBennett look-alike was still there, but I figured I'd better get back to work.

Turned out I didn't need to hurry. When I got back to Slim's, the place was nearly empty. I took a seat next to Flo at the counter.

"What should I do next?"

"Relax," she said. "Everything's under control for now."

"What will my hours be?" I asked Flo.

"We really need help on the weekends," she said. "But you might need to fill in during the week, too."

Weekends? When would I see Ryan? He had practice almost every day, and if I had to work nights, I'd never see him.

"Mornings or evenings?" I asked. I didn't have to say yes, I reminded myself.

To my relief, Flo said, "Mornings, especially Saturdays. As early as you can get here. You'll be pitching in with whatever—waiting tables, kitchen prep, maybe even cooking."

I didn't want to be one of those girls whose life completely revolved around her boyfriend, but I was glad I'd have some time to spend with Ryan.

Another question occurred to me. "And what should I wear?"

Flo shrugged. "We don't have a dress code here. Obviously."

I glanced at her T-shirt, which had WOMEN WHO PAY THEIR OWN RENT DON'T HAVE TO BE NICE on the front. Obviously, indeed.

"Just wear the kind of thing you usually wear," Flo said. "And Slim will give you an apron."

A minute later, the entire football team walked into Slim's. The jukebox stopped and suddenly went into "Leader of the Pack" by the Shangri-Las. Very funny.

Ryan's face lit up when he saw me. "I was just going to call you to see if you wanted to meet us here for lunch. Samantha and some of the other cheerleaders are on the way."

I explained that I'd be working there, and then got busy taking their orders.

Bane Paxton's little brother, Wolfgang, grabbed my arm. "Hey, cutie, what's your name?"

Ryan growled low in his throat, but I sent him a look to let him know I could handle a freshman.

"Let go of me if you want to keep that hand," I said, smiling politely.

Bane's brother said, "Hey, I saw the way you were looking at me. You like what you see, right? Wanna taste of lupine love?"

He said it under his breath, but Sean heard him. "In your dreams, Wolfgang," Sean said. "She's Ryan's girlfriend, hairball, so I'm guessing she was looking at him, not at some freshman squid who isn't even on the football team."

Wolfgang had a mop of bushy black hair, which stood up in every direction and smelled musty like he'd been left in a damp room too long. Not my type at all, even if I wasn't so into Ryan.

The tension ratcheted up a notch.

Ryan said, "And if you don't take your hands off her—"

"What?" the guy said, but he removed his hand from my wrist. A minute later, he got up and went to the jukebox.

I stared after him for a moment. "When did Bane's little brother turn into such a pain?" I said. Bane Paxton was in Poppy's graduating class and dated Elise Wilder. Like the Wilders, the Paxtons were shifters. I knew from my experience with Ryan that teenage werewolves could get a little aggressive sometimes, but Wolfgang seemed to be extra jerky. My wrist ached where he had grabbed me.

"He's got a chip on his shoulder," Ryan said. "He didn't make the team. If he tries anything . . ."

"He won't," I said. "Besides, I can take care of myself."

A group of Nightshade High cheerleaders came into the restaurant. They pulled up a table next to the football players, and suddenly the rush was on again.

Flo took pity on me and helped me out. My classmates were not going easy on me just because it was my first day, although Rachel was gentle when she pointed out that she had ordered the salad and Sean was the one who'd ordered the double-deluxe extra rare cheeseburger with fries.

Wolfgang had disappeared, so I decided it was safe to invite everyone to the party. It would save me making a bunch of phone calls. "Hey, Samantha," I said. "We're having a beach party on Saturday."

Rachel's head swiveled around. "Everyone's invited," I said, and smiled at her. I really liked Rachel, even though we had the same taste in guys.

The diner emptied out a couple of hours later.

Finally, the day was over and I grabbed an iced latte and sat on a stool at the counter. It had been hours since I'd had any caffeine or chocolate, two dietary essentials in my book.

"How do you do it?" I asked Flo.

"You get used to it," Flo replied. "Go home and soak your feet. And buy some shoes with good arch support."

I went home and soaked my feet as Flo had suggested, but I didn't know that it would be my last moment of peace for the next few weeks. My life was about to get much more complicated. So complicated that aching feet were the least of my worries.

CHAPTER FOUR

It was finally the day of the beach party. I'd spent a couple of hours cooking the night before, and Poppy and Candy were going to pack the food and take it to the beach while I was at work.

At the diner, I went back to the kitchen, but there was a stranger there with Slim. She was a short, curvy young woman with horn-rimmed glasses and blond hair, which was dyed with purple stripes.

It was clear, from her flirtatious giggles and Slim's low laugh, that I was interrupting, so I headed for the front.

"Who is that with Slim?" I asked Flo.

"That's Natalie, his new girlfriend," she replied. "She's a witch."

"You don't like her?"

Flo laughed. "No, I mean she's a real witch. She goes to grad school in Oregon, but she spends summers at her grandma's house in Nightshade. You'll be seeing her a lot this summer."

I nodded. "Need any help out here?"

Flo gave me a list of jobs and I started with the ketchup bottles, which needed refilling every morning.

I cheated a bit, when no one was looking, and used my powers to clean the coffee urn and to scrub the stainless steel.

I stared out the window as I worked. The sun was shining, and it was shaping up to be a perfect beach day.

A few minutes later, Slim's girlfriend came to the counter. "Hi, I'm Natalie Mason. We didn't introduce ourselves earlier. I was a little preoccupied." She let out a breathy laugh that made me glad my boss was invisible. Whatever they'd been doing in the kitchen, I didn't want to see it.

"I'm Daisy," I replied. A thought struck me. "Are you related to Mrs. Mason? I think her first name is Matilda?" I asked her. Mrs. Mason was the president of my mom's garden club. She always wore orthopedic shoes and a jogging suit. Mom had often wondered how Mrs. Mason managed to grow roses the size of a bread plate every year.

I finally figured it out when I saw her with her wand at a Nightshade City Council meeting. The city council was made up of members of Nightshade's thirteen founding families—all paranormal beings. They kept tabs on any weirdness in town.

"She's my grandma," Natalie replied. "How do you know her?"

"She and my mom belong to the same garden club," I said. "She grows beautiful roses."

Natalie paused, then said, "Yes, she really has a green thumb. She can make anything grow."

Of course she could, since she was a wand-carrying witch; and according to Flo, Natalie had the same talents.

"I didn't catch your last name," she said.

"Oh, I'm sorry." I held out a hand. "It's Giordano."

She grabbed it and shook my hand vigorously. "You're Daisy Giordano?"

Natalie dropped my hand and gave me a hug. "Oh, it's so great to meet you. I've heard so much about you and your family."

My mom's psychic powers, especially, were notorious even outside Nightshade. "Uh, that's great," I said. I didn't know what else to say. Natalie's enthusiasm made me squirm, so I changed the subject.

"What's your grandma planting right now? Do you help her in the garden?" I didn't know very much about gardening, but I needed a topic of conversation.

She blinked and I noticed that her eyes were brown rimmed in yellow.

"That's difficult to explain," she said, then quickly changed the subject. "How do you like working here? Isn't it great working for Slim?"

Natalie sounded a little hero-worshipy about Slim. She looked to be in her twenties, about Flo's age. I wondered briefly

33

how old Slim was, but then we were slammed by the breakfast crowd and I had no more time for idle romantic speculation.

When my shift was over, I felt slightly grubby and smelled like sweat and scrambled eggs. I changed into a bathing suit and cover-up, braided my hair, and slathered on sunscreen, then headed back to the kitchen.

"Slim, can you spare a couple of strawberry pies?" I asked. "I'll pay for them, of course. I just wanted to make sure I wouldn't leave you short."

"Take as many pies as you need," he said. "And make sure Flo gives you the employee discount."

"Thanks, Slim!" He was pretty cool for a boss. Maybe working at the diner all summer wouldn't be so bad after all. I paid for the pies and got a 50 percent discount. A definite perk.

When I made it to the beach, almost everyone we'd invited was already there, plus several tagalongs.

It looked like there was plenty of food, even though I hadn't counted on such a big crowd. There were pyramids of hamburger and hot dog buns, jumbo containers of potato salad, and chips. Ryan was busy manning the barbecue, which was already covered with huge slabs of meat. From the amount of food I saw, it looked like we were expecting the entire town.

Poppy bounded over wearing the new pink skull bikini she had gotten at Tete de Mort, the store where Samantha worked. "Guess what, Daisy?" she said. "On the way over here today, I got a job!"

I looked my sister over skeptically. "You must have made quite an impression at your interview," I said.

"Very funny," Poppy said, crossing her arms over her chest. "It wasn't a planned thing," she explained. "Candy and I stopped by that little concession stand by the boardwalk to get her a candied apple and noticed that they had a Help Wanted sign. So I got to chatting with the owner and she hired me on the spot. I start tomorrow."

"Congrats!" I said. "Can you get me an employee discount on chocolate bars?"

"Is chocolate all you think about?" Poppy said, as she headed off to continue her volleyball game.

Chocolate most certainly was not *all* I thought about. I smiled to see my boyfriend coming to meet me.

He took the pies out of my hands and gave me a quick kiss. "How was work?" he asked.

"Okay," I said. "Slim said he might let me do some prep work in the kitchen next week."

"What's Slim like, anyway?" Ryan asked.

I wasn't sure if I was supposed to say anything about Slim's being see-through.

"He's . . ." I floundered with my words. "He's . . . different. Sometimes I don't even notice he's there."

Elise Wilder and Bane Paxton came up to where Ryan and I stood. I was wiggling out of my cover-up, although not without some misgivings. We'd eaten lots of delicious desserts in Italy and I wasn't sure my body was exactly beach-ready. But I shrugged and tossed the cover-up to the ground. I wasn't going to let a few extra pounds stop me from having a good time.

"Thank you for inviting us," Elise said.

"I'm glad you could come," I said.

Elise's eyes focused on something behind me. She stiffened. "You invited Penny?"

"No, I didn't." Penny Edwards, Nightshade High's number one gossip, was here? I turned and looked. Penny wasn't easy to take, except in very small doses. Normally, I'd rather stake a vampire than talk to her, but I'd seen another side of her at prom.

"Daisy," Penny said. "I hope it's okay that I came." Gone was Penny's usual garish clothing. She wore a swimsuit in a subdued color, and her normal nasally tone was sweeter than usual.

I summoned a smile. "Of course."

"Can I help with anything?" she continued. "I brought you a cake." She held out an enormous bakery box.

"Thank you, Penny." She continued to stand there docilely. I exchanged a look with Elise. "Why don't you put it on the picnic table with the other desserts?"

Why was Penny being so nice? We'd had a little moment of friendliness at prom, but this affable Penny was unexpected.

I waited for a snarky comment, but she just beamed at me.

"Great. I really like that suit you're wearing, Daisy. It looks really cute on you."

What was going on with Penny? She was a social climber, for sure, but she had never considered me worth her time.

Elise and I exchanged glances as Penny bounced over to the table with her cake. A minute later, she had cut an enormous slice of it and had shoved it in her mouth. I knew for a fact that Penny hadn't let carbs touch her lips since the sixth grade. She noticed my gaze and grinned at me. A little dribble of frosting ran down her chin. She certainly was happy. Creepily happy.

"Penny's acting . . . a little unusual," I said. "Will you keep an eye on her?"

Elise frowned. "Yes, yes, I will." Penny had moved on to the chocolate brownies. I was dumbfounded by her table manners, or more accurately, lack thereof.

Poppy's friend Candy came up to where we all stood. "What is there to drink?" she asked. "I'm parched!"

"Let me get you something," Ryan said.

"After that," Poppy said, "I want to say hi to the guys. The single ones."

For a minute, she sounded like the old Poppy.

There was a cooler full of sodas right behind us. Ryan handed me a soda—one with caffeine, of course—then gave Poppy and Candy the diet sodas they requested.

"I just remembered," I said. "I brought fresh lemonade."

It was in an insulated container, but it wasn't quite cold

enough. While I was adding some ice, Wolfgang made a beeline for me.

"If it isn't my favorite waitress."

I ignored the leer that accompanied his comment, but he moved closer until he was definitely invading my personal space. My bikini suddenly felt entirely too revealing, so I grabbed my cover-up and threw it on, hoping he'd finally go away.

He didn't. Instead, he poured a glass of lemonade and gulped it down. He threw the plastic cup on the ground.

I glared at him. I hate people who litter.

"You're thirsty today, little Wolf," Ryan said.

Wolfgang wiped his forehead. "Yeah, it's a hot day. What of it?"

The air suddenly felt a lot denser. Ryan bared his teeth. "You're right," he said reasonably, and poured a glass of lemonade for himself.

A trickle of sweat inched down Wolfgang's face.

Ryan took a long drink, then he very elaborately threw his cup into the trash, where it belonged. He looked at Wolfgang levelly. "You know what to do."

Without another word, Wolfgang deflated. He bent over and picked up his trash. He started to retreat, until one of his cronies snickered.

I thought a scene had been averted, until I heard Ryan's next words: "Who invited you?" I was startled by his pugnacious tone.

Wolfgang bristled. "It's a public beach. We have as much right to be here as you do."

"Look out," Elise said. She took me by the arm and led me a few feet away.

"What?"

"Werewolves are territorial," she explained.

"But the full moon is weeks away."

"Doesn't matter," she said. "Remember, they are both young Weres and still learning control."

But Ryan managed to control himself, saying, "Whatever." He then shrugged and walked away, but Bane's little brother tackled him when he wasn't looking. Ryan and Wolfgang instantly became a pile of snapping, snarling testosterone.

Although Wolfgang had the element of surprise, Ryan was bigger and stronger. And seriously angry.

Sean and Bane managed to pull them apart, however, and Bane hustled his little brother toward the parking lot, presumably to send him home.

Meanwhile, Sean was guiding a still-seething Ryan away from the party, but Ryan twisted away from him. "Stay out of it, Sean," he snapped.

"Oh, that's how it is, is it?" Sean replied, and took off down the beach.

In a split second, Ryan had regained his calm and realized he'd hurt his best friend's feelings.

"Sean, I'm sorry, man," he said, but Sean kept walking.

Ryan trailed after him, still apologizing as they went out of sight.

Samantha appeared by my side. "I hope those two work out their differences," she said.

"What do you mean?" I asked. "Sean and Ryan are best friends."

"Yeah," Samantha said. "But, Daisy, even you can't deny Ryan's been secretive these past few months." She paused, seeing the offended look on my face, then explained, "Sean just feels like Ryan is shutting him out or something."

That's exactly how I felt before Ryan told me that he was a Were.

"I'll talk to him," I said, then sighed.

I thought about what Sam had said, while I toasted a marshmallow over the fire pit. There had been major drama leading up to the prom, and even though Ryan was gaining more control over his wolflike tendencies, he could still be really moody sometimes. His behavior must have been puzzling to people who didn't know he was a Were. But it was up to Ryan to tell people when he was ready. And apparently he still hadn't let Sean in on the big secret.

Ryan and Sean were gone a long time, but when they finally made it back to the party, Ryan was smiling and laughing with Sean, his dark mood evidently forgotten.

Ryan sat down next to me and slung an arm around my shoulder.

"Everything okay?" I asked.

"I'm fine. I just needed to cool off a little."

"What was that all about?"

"I lost my temper," he admitted. "Wolfgang has been bugging me. And I don't like how he looks at you. But it's all good."

"Hey, Ryan," I said softly. "Did you happen to tell Sean . . ."

"Nah," he said. "This is a party. Didn't want to ruin it with anything heavy. I'll tell him soon, though."

I looked across the fire. Sean was sitting next to Samantha and looking happy enough, but a shadow fell on his expression as the firelight flickered. I knew how it felt when someone you cared about was hiding something from you. I just hoped Ryan wouldn't keep his best friend in the dark for much longer.

CHAPTER FIVE

On Monday night, I was surprised to get a call from Natalie. "Daisy, I have a big favor to ask you," she said. "Could you teach me to cook?"

"You want to learn to cook from me?"

"Yes," she said. "I want to surprise Slim by cooking him a special meal, and I've never cooked anything more complicated than Top Ramen."

I laughed. "Sure, do you have something in mind?"

"Beef Wellington," she replied. "It's Slim's favorite dish."

It was a little ambitious for a beginning cook, but I'd try to walk her through it. We made plans to meet at her grandmother's the next evening. I'd never been inside Mrs. Mason's house, although I'd seen the enormous garden and greenhouse in her backyard plenty of times.

Natalie met me at the door. "I went shopping in San Carlos at that gourmet food store and got everything we need," she said. "And while I was there, I saw this." She waved a piece of paper in my face.

"What is it?"

She handed it to me. "It's a cooking contest," she said. "You enter your favorite family recipe. I thought of you right away."

"Oh," I said. "I've never cooked for anybody besides family and friends before."

"And the best part is that the grand prize is a trip to Le Cordon Bleu in Paris."

Paris? That was a great prize.

"Thanks, Natalie," I said. "Maybe I will enter." I slipped the flyer into my purse. I'd fill it out as soon as I got home. Otherwise, I'd never get it done.

Natalie and I were in the kitchen preparing the tenderloin when I noticed a large tabby cat observing us silently from the top of the cabinets. Its watchful green eyes were intimidating.

"I didn't know you had a cat," I said.

"That's my familiar," Natalie said. "I wish he could go everywhere with me, but unfortunately they don't allow animals in the diner. Not even magical ones."

Natalie reached up and gave the cat a bit of meat, and he purred gratefully. It made me miss my old cat, Midnight. But it turned out that she was a shifter and therefore not an ideal pet.

We heard Mrs. Mason arrive home.

"There's Grandma now," Natalie said. "C'mon. I'll formally introduce you."

We walked into the living room, where Mrs. Mason stood.

She was talking on her cell phone. "But you have to come help me with this," she said into the phone. "I have clothes for the—" She paused as she caught sight of us. "I'll call you back."

"Grandma, this is Daisy Giordano. I think you know her mother."

Mrs. Mason frowned. "I didn't realize you had company." There was a huge bag at her feet. She wore a purple tracksuit with a row of fake flowers hot-glued to the collar. I wondered where she kept her wand stashed in those sweats.

"Daisy's teaching me to cook," Natalie said.

"I don't see why you won't just whip something up the easy way," her grandmother said, making a motion with her hand.

Apparently I had been staring curiously, because Mrs. Mason frowned at me. "Donation items," she said, "for my charitable work."

It was her outfit I'd been focused on, but now I realized that the bag at her feet was filled with men's clothing. "Oh," I said lamely. "That's nice."

"I'll leave you two girls alone," Mrs. Mason said, picking up the bag. "I'll be in the greenhouse, Natalie, and I'm not to be disturbed."

"Yes, Grandma," she replied obediently.

After Mrs. Mason left, Natalie explained, "Grandma is extremely touchy about the greenhouse. Even I'm not allowed inside."

I briefly wondered why she was taking the clothes with her

to do her gardening, but soon got caught up in teaching the basics to Natalie. She hadn't been kidding when she said she'd never cooked before.

As the pastry for the beef Wellington baked, we chatted about her life back home. Natalie revealed that she'd spent most of her time at school ever since her father died a few years back.

"That's awful," I said. I knew how it felt to lose a dad. "If you don't mind me asking, how did he die?"

Natalie took a deep breath. "He was murdered," she said. "By people who found out about his magical abilities. They thought he was a freak. So they killed him."

I grimaced. I had never heard anything so awful. It was hard to imagine people could be so hateful. "I'm so sorry, Natalie," I said. I wondered if the people who killed her dad could have been part of the Scourge. It was their goal to wipe out paranormals of all kinds.

She wiped away a single tear and smiled again. "Well, things can only get better, right?" she said. "My grandma's the only family I have left. That's why I'm spending the summer in Nightshade."

"Did they ever catch who killed him?"

Natalie shook her head. "My grandmother even alerted the Nightshade City Council when the threats against him started, but by the time the council reached him, it was too late."

It was past eleven when we finished and Natalie walked me to the door.

"Thanks so much," she said. "I think I've got it now. Sorry about your arm, though."

She'd accidentally set down a hot pan a little too close to where I was working and my arm had been burned. "It's nothing," I said. "Don't worry about it."

"I'm such a klutz," she said with a moan. "Grandma says I can't do anything right."

I was beginning to not like Mrs. Mason. Natalie, on the other hand, was a sweetheart and I could see why Slim was smitten.

"It's nothing," I assured her. "Just a little mark, really. It doesn't even hurt." In truth, it was throbbing, but Natalie looked relieved and headed back inside.

As I stood on the porch, rummaging in my purse for a Band-Aid, a strange green glow appeared. It seemed to be coming from the back of Mrs. Mason's house.

Snooping was second nature to me, I guess, because I didn't hesitate to investigate. Walking closer, I could see that the light was coming from the greenhouse. I was surprised she was working on her plants so late.

I crept closer and peered through the doorway. The glass building was stuffed to the gills with plants and flowers, which spilled out of containers. Ferns the size of grown men lined one side. There was moss on the floor and a thick moist heat made it hard for me to breathe. I heard a low groaning noise and stepped into the room.

Dense foliage partially obstructed my view, but I could see that Mrs. Mason was bent over something on a long wooden table. She mumbled and green sparks flew from the object.

Without thinking, I gasped, then hid behind a large fern. Mrs. Mason stiffened and wheeled around. She peered into the darkness. I told myself there was no way she could see me, but I felt as if her eyes were boring into me.

"Who is there?" she cried. She raised her wand menacingly, and for a second, she didn't look like the pleasant elderly woman who took prizes for her roses every year. There were deep lines in her face and her eyes held a dangerous gleam. I didn't move and a minute later, she went back to her work.

I slipped out while her back was turned, then ran all the way home. What exactly was Mrs. Mason growing in her greenhouse?

Had I really heard a groan? I'd decided that my imagination was getting the better of me. Mrs. Mason was probably just working on her flowers with magic. The explanation satisfied me and I put the incident out of my mind.

CHAPTER SIX

I was doing laundry on Thursday when my cell rang. I checked the number of the caller. It was my boyfriend, and a call from him always made my day better.

"We haven't been to the new outdoor theater yet. Let's go tonight," Ryan suggested. "Just the two of us."

I considered the idea. Milk Duds, a dark night, and Ryan. What's not to love?

"Sounds good. What's playing?" The owner of Nightshade's new outdoor movie theater had a fondness for old horror movies, Vincent Price, Lon Chaney, Bela Lugosi, and stuff like that.

So I wasn't surprised when Ryan said, "*House of Dracula*."

I smiled. "It's a date."

The movie was crowded. A big screen was set up on the pier, close to the Snack Shack, where Poppy worked. The audience members brought blankets and low chairs. People in Nightshade tended to drift in after spending the day at the beach. Or in a coffin. Whichever. I noticed a vampire couple sitting on a blood red blanket in the front.

I was getting pretty good at telling a paranormal from a norm. The lack of color in the couple's skin was a giveaway that they were of the undead persuasion. And the female vampire was absolutely stunning. She bore a strong resemblance to a silent-movie star from over a hundred years ago. Who knows? Maybe it was her.

"Want something?" Ryan asked. "I could use a soda." The Snack Shack stayed open late for the summer movie nights.

"Mmm. Milk Duds and a large root beer, please."

While he was gone, I people-watched. Obviously, Poppy wasn't working at the concession stand, because I saw her arrive with Candy and put a blanket down right next to a group of cute guys. I waved to them and then said hi to a couple of girls from the cheerleading squad. I relaxed in my lawn chair while I waited for Ryan to get back with the goodies.

My sense of contentment was shattered a minute later, when I saw Wolfgang Paxton leading a group of rowdy guys to the front. To my surprise, I saw that Sean was at the back of the pack. *What is he doing hanging out with those creeps?* I thought, then I realized, they were all on the football team.

Everyone except Wolfgang, of course. And why was Wolfgang their leader?

Unfortunately, there was no sign of Bane, who seemed to be able to keep his brother in line.

Wolfie shoved his way in front of a little girl and knocked a box of candy out of her hand. He didn't even pause to say sorry, and all the rest of the guys followed without looking her way. All the guys except Sean, who picked up the candy and handed it to her before continuing on his way.

Sean was wearing a light shirt and shorts. His muscles looked like they had muscles. I frowned. He'd bulked up a lot since I'd seen him last.

Wolfie and his crew flopped down behind the vampire couple. Wolfie leaned forward and whispered something to the female vampire. Her shoulders stiffened, but she kept her gaze firmly on the screen, even though the previews hadn't started yet.

"Did I miss anything?" Ryan handed me my soda and box of candy.

"Not on the screen, but Wolfie looks like he's about to start something."

We watched as Wolfie reached out and touched the female vampire's hair. She ignored him, but the male vampire turned in a flash, his fangs bared and fists clenched.

In response, Wolfie and his pals jumped to their feet. Fortunately, an usher came by and politely suggested that they find a spot far away from the couple.

After a tense second, Wolfie got up and moved several rows back from the couple. His buddies followed.

Ryan leaned forward until his breath tickled my ear. "That usher's dad is the head of a very powerful Were pack outside San Carlos. Even Wolfie's not stupid enough to mess with him."

Apparently, Ryan was plugged into the whole Were community now. It gave me a pang to realize he had a whole life that I wasn't a part of, not really.

He was right, though. At least it seemed as though Wolfie had calmed down. The movie started without any further interruptions.

But halfway through the movie, Wolfie started throwing candy at the vampire couple. There were a couple of loud snickers. The male vampire turned around, and in the dark, his eyes were lit with a red fire.

"I advise you to stop that, Paxton cub," he said in a loud voice. "If I didn't know who your father and brother were, your throat would already be torn out."

Wolfie stood and his cronies followed suit. All but Sean, who looked like he wanted to be anywhere but where he was.

"This is the kind of trouble we don't need," Ryan said. "I'll be right back."

The entire movie audience held its collective breath as Wolfie made a slight movement toward the vampires.

I had to do something. No time like the present to practice a little telekinesis. I concentrated and Wolfie's extra-large soda flew out of his hand and landed upside down on his head, showering him with icy cola.

Ryan threw an amused glance my way but continued to where Wolfgang and the others were. "You," he said in a measured voice. "Out." He grabbed Wolfie's arm and twisted it behind his back. His gaze encompassed the rest of the team. "All of you. Now. And don't come back."

Ryan marched Wolfie up the pier. Wolfgang's eyes burned into mine as he passed me, but he didn't say a word.

Sean was the last in line. I grabbed his arm. "What are you doing with those guys, Sean?" I knew they were all on the football team together, but Sean was hanging with—well, frankly, the creeps of the bunch. And besides, Sean was a senior and Wolfie was a freshman.

He shrugged off my arm. "Stay out of it, Daisy."

"Sean!"

But he ignored me and continued after his buddies. I waited a couple of minutes and then followed. I wanted to make sure Ryan was okay. He was a werewolf, but so was Wolfgang and who knew who else in that little group.

There was no sign of them on the other end of the pier, but I caught a glimpse of Ryan standing behind the Snack Shack.

"Is everything okay?" I asked. Wolfgang and his group were gone, all except Sean, who was looking down at the ground when I approached.

"Everything is fine," Ryan assured me. "I just need five minutes alone with Sean."

I grabbed his arm and pulled him a few feet away, hopefully out of Sean's earshot.

"You're not going to fight him?"

"Of course not. He's my best friend. I'm just going to try to talk some sense into him."

He gave me a quick kiss and then I went back to my seat, but it took Ryan longer than five minutes to rejoin me. In fact, the movie was almost over by the time he slid into the lawn chair next to me.

"Sorry," he said. "I didn't mean for that to take so long." He looked grim.

"Is Sean okay?" I whispered.

"Stubborn, but he's okay. I think I got through to him about being a little more selective about who he hangs out with." Ryan took my hand. "I'm really sorry, Daisy. I'll make it up to you."

The movie ended a few minutes later, but I hadn't really been paying attention, anyway. I was more concerned about Ryan, and how could I be mad at him for trying to help Sean?

I didn't want our date to end on such a down note. "I'll forgive you if you forgive me."

Ryan looked startled. "For what?"

"I ate all the Milk Duds. And the popcorn," I joked, and was relieved when he cracked a smile. It was a small one, but it was a beginning.

"Then you can buy me a slice of pie at Slim's," he replied.

"As much as I love that place, I've been spending all my time there. I'm pretty sure we still have some apple pie left at my house. And no one's home."

"Even better," Ryan said, as we walked out of the theater. And it was.

CHAPTER SEVEN

It was Friday night. I had decided to stay home and hang out with Poppy, who still had days awash in tears, mourning the loss of Gage.

Since I was staying home, Ryan had planned a night out with the guys. Rose was working late at the lab, so Poppy and I headed to the video store.

"How about this one?" Poppy said. She gestured toward one of the more gory selections in the horror section.

I wrinkled my nose. "How about something with less slash and more suspense?"

Poppy wandered into the next aisle. A minute later, she came back waving a DVD. "We're going to watch this tonight."

I peered at the movie in her hand. "*Truly, Madly, Deeply?* What's it about?"

"You'll love it," she replied, but she didn't meet my eyes.

I read the description on the back. "A ghost? You want to watch a movie about a doomed love affair with a ghost?"

"I miss him, Daisy," she said softly, "but I know he's not coming back. As a ghost or anything else."

I frowned. "I don't think—"

"It's not any different from when Rose watched *An American Werewolf in London* over and over that time she and Nicholas broke up," Poppy pointed out.

My sister and Nicholas had broken up when they were high school sweethearts. Rose didn't know it at the time, but he had broken up with her because he was having a hard time dealing with being a Were, not because he didn't care about her. They were back together and seemed to have resolved all their relationship issues.

I couldn't resist Poppy's pleading eyes. "Okay, but I get to pick one, too."

"The werewolf movies are over there," she said.

I smiled to see Poppy kidding around again, but on impulse, I grabbed a couple of older werewolf movies and then we checked out and headed for home.

Poppy wanted to watch *Truly, Madly, Deeply* first, so I popped it into the machine and settled on the couch next to her. By the end of the movie, we both had reached for the tissues.

I clicked off the movie. "You know what we need?"

"More tissues?" Poppy joked, but her eyes were still watery.

"No, chocolate," I said. "Let's make brownies. With the good chocolate."

We still had some of the chocolate we'd brought back from Europe, although, thanks to me, not very much of it was left.

But it was enough for me to whip up some truly delicious brownies.

"You know, I've really been enjoying cooking the old-fashioned way lately," I said as I stirred the batter. "But my telekinesis might come in handy at Slim's during a rush."

"Have you tried to hone your powers at all?"

I thought about her question. "Not really. I've been busy." I hoped she didn't ask doing what. Summer was for relaxing, right? "I did dump soda on Wolfgang the other night at the movies, using my powers."

"I *thought* that was you," she said.

"He deserved it," I replied.

She chuckled. "Of course he did, but it doesn't pay to get rusty," Poppy said. "Especially not in Nightshade."

She had a point. I poured the batter into the pan and put it into the oven, then gave her a beater to lick.

"Why don't we practice now? We have about half an hour before the brownies are done."

We went outside, where the night sky was sharp with stars. The moon was out, but I noted with relief that it wasn't full yet.

I faced Poppy. "So, what now?" She'd been helping me train to improve the control of my telekinesis ever since we'd found out about it, but it had been awhile since I'd put in any real work.

"Let's try something different," she said. "Try to open the front door, using your mind."

It took me about fifteen minutes, which meant I really *was* rusty, but I finally managed to do it.

"You're horribly out of practice," Poppy scolded me. "You've got to work at it, Daisy."

As she was lecturing me, I heard the howl of a wolf, which was not all that unusual in Nightshade, considering our werewolf population. It was followed by several other howls, closer this time.

I stared up at the moon. "Look, it's not even full."

She shrugged. "No big deal. Rose isn't with Nicholas. She's on campus. And besides, Nicholas has a lot of control."

"Yes, but Ryan's out with the guys tonight," I said. As a new werewolf, the last thing my boyfriend should be doing was socializing this close to a full moon. He hadn't completely figured out how to handle the transformation yet, and teen wolves often shifted even when the moon wasn't full.

A minute later, the howls had turned to snarls and the sounds were coming closer. "It sounds like they're chasing something."

"It's not like they're right next door or anything," she said.

But she was wrong. I caught the gleam of red eyes in the darkness.

"Poppy," I said, "I think it's time we went inside. Now."

"But we just . . ." She trailed off when she saw my face.

58

There was a snarl and then a werewolf appeared out of the bushes about twenty feet in front of us. We weren't entertaining just one werewolf. From my count, it looked like a whole pack. I tried to shake off my paralyzing fear.

"Move slowly," I cautioned her, but Poppy was already bolting for the door.

She'd nearly reached it when a blur of fur and snapping teeth launched itself at her back. I put up a hand, and the next thing I knew, a heavy flowerpot flew across the yard and hit the wolf squarely on the nose. He dropped to the ground, panting and whimpering, but out of the corner of my eye, I saw another wolf creep forward.

I sprinted to the door and made it inside with seconds to spare. I slammed the door and turned the lock, and Poppy and I stood trembling in our foyer. We waited, but there was only silence outside. Then we finally heard the sound of the pack running into the night. I sagged against the door frame.

Poppy took a shaky breath. "What the heck was that all about?" she said.

"I don't know," I said. "But I think they were young wolves—teenagers maybe. They have to be. Why else would they shift when it's not even a full moon?" There was something still puplike about a couple of the wolves.

"There aren't that many young werewolves in Nightshade, are there?"

I thought about it, then counting on my fingers, I listed them. "There's Nicholas, Bane Paxton and his little brother, Wolfgang, Elise Wilder, and Ryan. That's all I can think of."

"That's only five," Poppy said. "But you saw a lot more, didn't you?"

I nodded. "I think there were at least eight of them."

"Maybe they're out-of-towners," Poppy offered.

A terrible thought occurred to me. "Or maybe . . ."

"What?"

"Maybe someone is increasing the werewolf population."

"How does that happen?"

I shrugged. My werewolf boyfriend hadn't been exactly forthcoming about the particulars.

"Ryan might know something," Poppy said.

"He'd never do something like that!" I defended him. "Nicholas, either."

"Of course not." Poppy rolled her eyes. "I meant that since Ryan is a werewolf, he might know or could help us find out more about it." She shuddered. "Those wolves were on the hunt. I don't know what I would have done if you hadn't hit that one when you did."

"I'll ask Ryan," I told her, "the first chance I get." I didn't want him to think I was a scaredy-cat, so I decided to tell him in the morning.

I didn't realize that it would be some time before I saw him again.

CHAPTER EIGHT

I called Ryan's house the next morning during my break at Slim's, but I got his answering machine. I tried his cell, too, but there was no answer. By the time I left work, he still hadn't returned my call. I tried not to get irritated. It was late in the afternoon when he finally called me back. Rose and Poppy were both still at work, so I jumped a little when the phone rang.

He sounded stressed.

"I'm in Orange County," he said.

"What?" I was startled. He hadn't mentioned any upcoming trips, but I did know that he had family there.

"My grandmother took a fall yesterday. Dad and I left Nightshade last night right before dinner."

I knew it hadn't been Ryan in the pack last night, but I was relieved to hear that he'd already been on the road when we saw the teen wolves.

"Is she okay?"

"She broke her hip and she's a little shaken up. The surgery went well, but Dad and I will be here at least a week or two."

"Is there anything I can do?" There was no way I was going to tell him about the teen werewolf pack, not now. He had enough on his mind.

"Just be careful, Daisy. And ask Nicholas for help if you need it."

"Nicholas? I can take care of myself."

"I know you can," he said gently. "But a little backup wouldn't hurt."

After I hung up with Ryan, I weighed my options. I couldn't prove for certain that Wolfie was the culprit, but talking to Nicholas might be good. If nothing else, he could give me a little insight about pack behavior.

I wandered into the kitchen and took down a mixing bowl. I always thought more clearly when I was cooking. I'd start with the dessert. I decided on fresh peach ice cream. Poppy loved ice cream of any kind and ice cream might tempt her appetite. She still wasn't eating enough.

I figured Rose and Poppy would be home from work soon, and sure enough, Rose walked in while I was getting out the ice cream maker.

"Rose, do you know the next time Nicholas is coming over?"

"We have a date tonight," she said.

Perfect timing. "Do you mind if I borrow him for a few minutes? I have some questions about pack behavior."

"Go right ahead," she said. "Is Ryan having problems or something?"

"No, it's not that." I told her about Wolfgang Paxton's obnoxious behavior and how Poppy and I had been cornered by the Were pack the night before.

"Daisy, this is serious," she said. "Remember, Nicholas didn't grow up in a pack, but he's done a lot of research. It sounds like there's a renegade pack on the loose in Nightshade."

"Why don't you invite Nicholas over for dinner?" I said. "I'll cook and then we can pick his brain."

"That's a great idea," Rose said. "We were just going to go to a movie or something, but he loves your cooking."

I felt a warm glow at her praise. I wasn't good at that many things, but I was the only one in my family who was good at cooking. Except my father, but he didn't count. Only the people who stayed with the family counted.

Rose went upstairs to prepare for her date and then Poppy came in as I was pouring the ice cream mixture into the maker.

"What's that?" she asked.

"Fresh peach ice cream," I replied. Her face lit up and I was glad I'd thought of it.

"Do you need any help?" she asked. "Otherwise, I'm going to go change." She was still in her work clothes.

"No, thanks," I replied. "I've got it handled."

Before she went to her room, she reminded me to practice.

I decided to try to get the pan I used for boiling pasta onto the stove using telekinesis. It worked out okay, except that I spilled a little water on the way over to the stove.

Since company was coming, I decided to jazz up what I'd planned for dinner. We had the ingredients to make a fresh tomato and herb bruschetta, so I got everything together and put it in the oven for an appetizer.

I wondered if I might like to be a professional chef someday. My senior year was coming up and I needed to start thinking seriously about my future. But first I had to figure out what was happening in Nightshade.

When the doorbell rang, I beat Rose to it.

"Hi, Nicholas," I said.

"Hi, Daisy." Nicholas smiled politely but looked behind me for Rose. Despite their rocky high school romance, he was clearly totally into my sister. Which was another reason I trusted Nicholas's judgment.

A timer rang in the kitchen, and I rushed to rescue the bruschetta from the oven. Rose and Nicholas followed me, and Poppy, attracted by the smell of baking bread, appeared a minute later. I transferred the appetizers onto a serving platter and then offered everyone some.

"These look great," Nicholas said. "Thanks so much for the dinner invite." He grabbed a piece of bruschetta and popped it into his mouth.

"I heard the phone ring earlier," I said to Poppy. "Was that Mom calling about her flight?"

"Yeah, she called," Poppy replied. "She's not coming home anytime soon. Her case is taking longer than expected."

I wondered what Mom was up to in Italy. She wasn't telling us the whole story, but there wasn't much I could do about it from Nightshade.

I changed the subject. "I made pasta, too. It's a new recipe. It should be ready in a minute." I knew pasta in the middle of summer was a little heavy, but Nicholas ate a lot and never seemed to gain an ounce.

"Why don't we take our plates and sit outside?" Poppy suggested.

We all grabbed our food and followed her suggestion. There was a little patio table in the backyard that was perfect for the four of us.

I couldn't very well grill Nicholas until I'd fed him, so I waited until he had eaten before asking him questions.

"Did Rose tell you about what happened to Poppy and me?" He nodded.

"Can you tell us a little bit about werewolf packs?"

"Normally, they're made up of families, related groups."

"Like the Wilders?" I asked.

"Exactly, although the Wilders are a little different because they have so many species of Were animals besides wolves in their family tree. There are two kinds of Weres, born and made. I have a suspicion that the Weres in the pack that attacked you were made."

"What makes you think that?"

"First of all, since they came after you on a night when there wasn't a full moon, they have to be new Weres who don't yet have the control that more experienced adult Weres do."

I nodded. "I know adult Weres have enough control that they change only when the moon is full. Plus, they were like puppies. Big feet and awkward, but still dangerous."

"And you say there were about eight of them? There aren't that many Were teenagers in Nightshade."

"Good point," I replied. "And besides, I don't really see Elise or Bane doing something like that, and I know it wasn't Ryan. He wasn't even in town."

"How are werewolves made?" Rose asked.

"It's a risky business," Nicholas said. "A werewolf finds a victim—sometimes willing, sometimes not—and bites him or her. Then the victim has to survive the change."

"Why would a Were want to do that to someone?" Poppy exclaimed. She sounded repulsed.

"Power," Nicholas said. "Or loneliness."

"It wouldn't surprise me if Wolfgang Paxton was involved," I said. "I've seen him be really nasty."

Poppy nodded. "Me, too."

Nicholas shook his head. "I would hope Wolfgang would know better than to do such a thing. Nevertheless, I'll tell the council members to keep an eye on him." He paused for another bite of pasta before he asked me, "Would you recognize the pack if you saw them again?"

"Definitely the wolf who seemed to be the leader." A troubling thought occurred to me. "Can a werewolf's bite be reversed?" I asked.

Nicholas looked startled. "I don't know."

"Because I have this weird feeling that Nightshade's football team has started howling at the moon."

Rose stared at me. "That's terrible."

"I know," I said. "Sean's on the football team and he's been acting really weird lately. And hanging out with Wolfgang Paxton, someone he couldn't stand before."

"Is there anything else that makes you think the team is involved?" Nicholas asked.

"They're all ordering their meat rare when they come to Slim's," I said. "And some of them have really bulked up."

"You should try to talk to Sean," Rose said. "Or ask Sam to."

"Ryan's Sean's best friend. He's already tried talking to him." I told him what had happened at the movie theater.

"Something's not right," Nicholas stated.

We had no idea what an understatement that was. Something was definitely wrong in Nightshade, and teen werewolves were only part of the problem.

CHAPTER NINE

After a few weeks of my working at the diner, Slim finally trusted me in the kitchen alone. At least, I *thought* he did. When your boss was an invisible man, it was hard to know for sure. I was getting more cooking shifts and fewer serving shifts. Of course, that could be because I drove Flo crazy when I made mistakes.

"Daisy," Slim said, "can I ask you a favor?"

"Sure." I faced the general direction of where I thought he was. Today it was fairly easy because he was chopping onions and I saw the knife flash.

I waited, but he didn't say anything. Finally, he cleared his throat. "Do you think you could handle the morning shift on your own for a while on Saturday?"

"Really?" I beamed at him. Then a thought struck me. "Is everything all right?"

"Yes, of course," he said. "But I'd rather you didn't say anything to Natalie. Or anyone else. Natalie gets anxious when I'm away. She'll notice eventually, but I'd appreciate it if you wouldn't call her attention to my absence."

"Of course," I said. "Does Flo know?"

I knew Natalie would kill me if she found out I'd been covering for her boyfriend. But he was a grown man, after all.

I wondered what kind of plans Slim had that he didn't want his girlfriend to know about, but I wasn't going to ask my boss about his love life. "What time should I be here?"

When my alarm rang at four A.M., I rolled over and groaned. I was faced with leaving for work in the pitch-black. The thought that only the vamps and me were up at this hour didn't help. At least until daybreak, that is.

I took a quick shower and got into some old clothes. They were still decent enough to wear to work, but I wouldn't be devastated if I stained, scorched, or sweated on anything I had on.

I braided my hair, then grabbed the car keys. Rose would drop off Poppy later in the morning. She'd be chomping at the bit to have the car, because she had to work later that day, but there was no way she was getting up early enough to take me to work. Being a two-car family was a pain sometimes, but it could be worse. We could all be harpies, like the Dickersons.

Although there was plenty of parking out front, I parked in the alley behind the restaurant. Slim preferred that staff park in the back.

The lights were already on at the donut shop across the street, and as I got out of the car, I breathed in the intoxicating smell of sugar and fried dough. My stomach growled loudly.

At least, I was hoping it was my stomach and not one of Nightshade's scarier residents when I noticed movement over by the dumpster.

A shabby figure stepped out of the shadows. A man, wearing dark clothes and a hat slung low, his mouth stuffed with yesterday's stale cinnamon rolls. He groaned as he chewed. It took me a minute to recognize the features under the wide-brimmed hat.

It was my father. The father I hadn't seen in years.

"Dad?" I said, shocked. The keys jangled as they dropped to the pavement. At the sound of my voice, he bolted away. I was unable to move as the knowledge swirled in my brain. My father was back in Nightshade and had made no attempt to contact his family.

After a long time, I picked up my keys with shaking hands and let myself into the diner. But I worried all through my shift. My previously elegant, immaculately clad dad had been dressed in a grungy pair of eighties parachute pants and a red flannel shirt. And he looked like he'd spent the last six years in a dumpster.

The diner was packed for breakfast, and I spent the next few hours sweating cinnamon rolls and black coffee. Gradually, the orders petered out and the restaurant emptied. I wandered to the front to get a coffee.

"You'd better take a break before the lunch rush starts." Flo patted a stool next to hers.

I was still consumed with second-guessing myself. Had it really been my father? And if it was, how on earth could I tell Mom?

Maybe the jukebox could shed a little light on the subject. It wasn't like other jukeboxes, any more than Nightshade was like other towns. The music player had given me plenty of clues solving other cases, but would it help me solve this one?

I handed Flo a five and asked for change in quarters. "Think Lil is still mad?" I asked, with a nod toward the jukebox.

She shrugged. "I think she missed you."

I fed my stack of quarters into the machine and punched in my selections, but there was no reaction. Not even my normal selections played. I was being given the silent treatment.

"Look, I'm sorry I was gone so long," I whispered. "But I really need your help."

Nothing. I checked my watch. It was almost eleven. Time to get ready for the lunch rush.

The door opened and Penny Edwards walked in.

"Hi, Penny," I said, eyeing her cautiously. Which Penny would I see today? The old Penny or the Penny at the beach?

"Giordano," she said, "I'm supposed to meet the rest of the

cheerleaders here. Can you show me to a table?" Penny seemed to be up to her usual tricks.

"We don't have a hostess here, Penny," I replied. "Just pick a spot and sit down."

She made it almost impossible to like her. There were no other customers, so I poured myself a cup of coffee and sat on one of the stools next to Flo. I wasn't going to fall all over myself to wait on Penny.

A few minutes later, other cheerleaders drifted in.

"Daisy, it's nice to see you," Rachel said. She gave me a big hug.

"I'm glad to see you," I said, hugging her back. Samantha and the rest of the squad came in, and since they were the only customers in the restaurant, I stayed and chatted.

"Could we *please* get some water? Like sometime today?" Penny demanded in a cold voice. I laid a restraining hand on Flo's arm. "I'll get it." I didn't want the whole squad getting kicked out of Slim's because of Penny's snotty attitude. Flo was capable of banishing them for much less.

I gave everyone glasses and set the water pitcher down in front of Penny. She gave me the cold shoulder, but her eyes held the gleam they got when she had good dirt. By the way she could barely suppress her glee when she looked at me, I knew that she was dying to say something about my sisters or me.

Flo took their order, which consisted of a dozen diet sodas, several salads, and a couple of orders of fries, so I headed back to the kitchen, but not before I heard Penny's raised voice. What had her in such a dither?

"He's in town, I'm telling you. My mother saw him in the parking lot of the grocery store and he looked like a bum or something."

"Shut up, Penny," Sam hissed, but for once, Penny ignored her.

"I'm telling you, it was Mr. Giordano."

So my father wasn't a figment of my imagination.

The jukebox chose that moment to end its silence and "Big Mouth Strikes Again" by the Smiths came on. Lil had finally forgiven me, but now I had bigger problems. If Penny had seen my dad, it was only a matter of time before news of his presence would be all over Nightshade.

CHAPTER TEN

When my shift ended, I rushed home to try to catch my sisters. I wanted them to hear the news about Dad from me instead of Penny's big mouth.

Rose and Poppy were hanging out in the living room. Poppy was in sweats, but Rose still wore a white lab coat, so she must have just gotten off work.

"Don't you ever take that thing off?" I teased.

Rose blushed. "I brought it home to wash it," she said, but I knew she was proud of her job at the university. Her boss, Dr. Franken, was a sort of superstar of the science world, always making headlines with her research in genetics.

"How was work?" Poppy asked, as she turned the pages of a fashion magazine.

I took a deep breath. "Fine," I said, losing my nerve. "How about you?"

"The weirdest thing happened," she replied.

"What?" Rose said.

"Remember Mrs. Wilder, Elise's grandmother?" Poppy said.

"She came by the stand and just started stuffing cotton candy in her mouth."

"You mean without paying?" It seemed out of character for the normally elegant matriarch to do something so vulgar.

"Exactly," Poppy said. "And she ate about five pounds of the stuff and then ran off with this dazed look on her face."

"I saw Mr. Krayson doing the same thing at the new donut shop," I said. It dawned on me that I'd seen several Nightshade residents scarfing sweets lately.

"That's strange even by Nightshade standards," Rose commented.

I saw my opening. "Well, here's something else strange," I began. "I didn't know if I should tell you, but Penny Edwards came into the diner today . . ." I paused, uncertain how to continue. "She was gossiping about Dad."

"When will they get sick of that old scandal!" Rose snapped.

"No, it's something new. Penny said Dad's in town," I blurted.

Poppy sat up. "Like she would recognize Dad if she saw him," she scoffed.

"No," I said slowly. "But I would."

I told them about the man I'd seen by the dumpster.

My sisters were obviously as stunned as I was by the news. "I'm not positive it was him," I admitted. "He didn't seem to recognize me." I tried to keep the hurt from my voice.

Rose said, "How could you not recognize your own father?"

"Six years is a long time," I said. "Do *you* remember everything from that long ago?"

"Yes, actually, I do," Rose said. "I have an excellent memory."

"Of course you do," I said. Rose was brilliant. And besides, she was fourteen when Dad disappeared. I was only twelve.

"I'm glad Mom's still in Italy," Poppy said. "She'd freak out if it turns out Dad is in town and just hasn't contacted us!"

The phone rang. It was Mom, calling long distance. I was really glad she couldn't see us, because I'm sure our faces all looked guilty.

We chatted for a few minutes about what she was doing in Italy, although she was evasive about the particulars of the case she was working on. Then she asked, "How's everything going there?"

I exchanged glances with my sisters, knowing we were thinking the same thing. We couldn't tell her, not yet.

But how much longer would we have before she came home and found out herself?

"Well, we were planning a welcome-home dinner. Any idea of how much longer you'll be there?" I was fishing for information, but it wasn't a bad idea, anyway. After all, Mom *had* been gone a long time. She deserved a warm welcome when she returned. I knew my best cooking efforts couldn't compare with the delicious meals we'd eaten in Italy, but I'd try to make Mom a truly memorable dinner.

I couldn't help but feel that maybe I was planning to cook a meal for her to silence my guilty conscience.

She sighed. "I'm afraid this case isn't winding up as quickly as I had anticipated. I'll be gone for at least another two weeks."

We had some time, then. And she wouldn't hear any rumors before then, not all the way in Italy. Besides, Mom had turned a deaf ear to gossip a long time ago. How else could she cope with the rumors that Dad had run off with another woman?

Part of me thought that I should tell Mom that Dad might be back in town, but I just couldn't get the words out.

That night I had the strangest dream, probably due to the lethal combination of guilt and nachos. In the dream, I saw my father's death. My sisters and I were there, but we did nothing. He was on the ground, in agony, and we were oblivious. Needless to say, I woke up gasping and sweaty, thinking that I'd have to ask Rose and Poppy to shed some light on my dream later, if they could. I'd heard about people who made predictions based on their dreams, but to my knowledge, no one in our family had that ability.

I did know that I needed to get to the diner, however, so I threw on my clothes and hurried to work.

The dream lingered with me throughout the day. Was it just a nightmare or a manifestation of a precognitive ability I didn't know I possessed?

After work, I was ambling along, tired from a long day, when

I spotted the man again, dressed in the same outfit as before, walking in the opposite direction. He carried a large donut box and kept sniffing at it.

Tired or not, I had to follow him, if only to figure out if it really was my father or just a look-alike. I trailed him from a good distance, but he never even looked in my direction.

When I breathed in the wonderful scent of flowers, I realized we were nearing Natalie's grandmother's garden.

Dad, or the stranger who resembled him, paused only a fraction of a second, then vaulted the picket fence around Mrs. Mason's backyard. I was working up the nerve to do the same, when I heard a car, which pulled into Natalie's driveway.

Mrs. Mason and Natalie were home and, by the looks on their faces, wondering what the heck I was doing camped out in their front yard.

"Hi, there," I said, smiling brightly as they got out of the car. "I dropped by on the spur of the moment. I thought you might like another cooking lesson."

From the corner of my eye, I saw the shrubs moving. I'm pretty sure Mrs. Mason saw the movement, too, although her expression didn't change. "I'm afraid that won't be possible. Another time, perhaps?" And with that, she took Natalie by the arm and marched into the house.

I looked around, but my father, or whoever he was, had vanished.

CHAPTER ELEVEN

My sisters and I planned to investigate our newly returned father but, unfortunately, had no idea of his whereabouts. You would think that in a town the size of Nightshade, it would be easy to locate a person, especially someone as infamous as Rafe Giordano, or his look-alike, as the case might be.

No one was talking, either, except to say stuff like "Daisy, I hear your father is back in town." But after inquiring, I would trace the rumor back to Penny Edwards.

I was beginning to think he was a figment of my imagination. Still, I was glad Mom wasn't home. I could only imagine the frenzy she would work herself into over this.

On Friday, Poppy and I were going to have lunch with Rose on campus. I was curious to see where she worked, and besides, we needed to talk about Dad in a place where half the town wouldn't overhear the conversation. The campus was usually fairly deserted in the summer, except for the smaller number of students taking summer classes.

We followed Rose's directions and found the parking lot she had indicated. After that, we made a long trek through the campus grounds. The campus was a hodgepodge of architectural styles. We saw everything from classic brick to seventies modern buildings.

Rose's lab was located in a building that had seen better days. The paint was peeling in spots and the windows needed washing. We went down a dingy, poorly lit hallway until we found the lab, but the door was locked.

"What should we do?" I said.

"Knock," Poppy suggested, "unless you want to send Rose a message telepathically. Or use my cell phone," she added dryly. I'd never thought about it before, but I wondered if it bugged Poppy that Rose and I could communicate nonverbally.

I tapped lightly on the door, but there was no answer.

"Pound on it," Poppy instructed. She whipped out her cell and punched in Rose's number. "She's not answering."

I knocked louder. Still no answer.

A moment later, the door opened a crack, revealing a woman in a lab coat. She had white cotton-candy hair, and I had to resist the impulse to take a bite.

"What do you want?" she snapped.

"Uh, we're here to see Rose Giordano," I said.

She didn't smile, but the severe look on her face lessened a bit. "You must be her sisters."

"Yes," Poppy said. "We're supposed to meet her for lunch. Is she here?" She peered through the doorway, but the woman stepped into the hallway and closed the door with a snap, effectively blocking Poppy's view.

"She left on an errand for me about an hour ago. I'm Dr. Franken."

After we had introduced ourselves, Rose came rushing up. She was carrying a stack of bakery boxes.

"Sorry I'm late," she said. To the professor she said, "I went to the Donut Hole, but they were already sold out."

Dr. Franken frowned. "I'm sure you did your best, my dear."

"I had to go to three different bakeries, but I managed to get everything on your list."

The professor cracked a smile. "Excellent." Without another word, she opened the door to the lab and disappeared behind it.

"Is she always like that?" Poppy said.

"She's a brilliant scientist," Rose said defensively. "She doesn't have time to stand around and chat."

"I'm sure she's very busy," I said, trying to avert a fight. "Let's eat. I'm starving."

Poppy pulled a compact out of her purse and applied a coat of lipstick. "How about the student center?" she suggested. "I want to get to know the campus. After all, I'll be going here in the fall."

On our walk to the student center, we passed a few people, but for the most part, campus seemed deserted.

Rose gave us a quick tour on the way. "Most of the food court is closed," she explained, "but a couple of the restaurants are still open."

"Why are they closed?" Poppy asked.

"Most of the students go home for the summer," Rose explained. "So it's mostly just faculty and staff left. Not too many people enroll in summer session."

"Oh," Poppy said. She looked crestfallen. "You mean I won't meet any frat guys today?"

"Doubtful," Rose said, smiling at me. It was nice to see Poppy show an interest in the opposite sex again.

We made our way to the food court and ordered sandwiches. There were plenty of empty tables, so we took a prime seat by a window, just in case one of Poppy's frat boys wandered by.

"I can't stay long," Rose said. "Dr. Franken has a project for me this afternoon."

After we had finished our lunches and Poppy was eying the dessert choices, I asked Rose something I'd been wondering about since we left the lab.

"What were all the bakery boxes for?"

She shrugged. "Dunno. Maybe she's hosting a breakfast tomorrow or something."

It would be kind of odd if she sent Rose out for donuts the day before a breakfast—especially since donuts were best fresh. Maybe Dr. Franken had a weird donut-based eating disorder or something.

"I thought you were her *lab* assistant," Poppy said, "not her personal assistant."

"I help with a lot of research," Rose protested. "And besides, Dr. Franken doesn't like to leave the lab."

"What? You mean like *ever*?" I thought that was a little odd.

"Hey, isn't that Mr. Bone?" Poppy said. She pointed to a tan, pudgy man in a polo shirt and khakis moving jerkily up the path toward the student center.

"What would he being doing on campus?" Rose said.

The door of the student center opened and Mr. Bone entered.

"Mr. Bone!" Rose waved at him, but he didn't even notice her. There was a snack kiosk in one corner and he headed for it without looking around. We watched in amazement as he ripped the wrappers off several candy bars and stuffed them into his mouth and then, as quickly as he'd come in, left, before the cashier could react.

Rose hurried after him, while Poppy and I went to the cashier. Poppy handed him a five-dollar bill. "Will this cover it?"

After the cashier handed Poppy her change, we raced after Rose and Mr. Bone. We caught up to her, but there was no sign of Mr. Bone anywhere.

Rose was talking on the phone, obviously to Nicholas.

"But I'm telling you, it was your dad," she said, then listened a minute.

"What's he saying?" Poppy said.

"Wait a minute," Rose said. "I can't talk to both of you at once."

Poppy made a face but quit talking.

"I think that's a good idea. Daisy and Poppy saw it, too. I'll see you tonight."

She hung up her phone.

"Well?" Poppy said.

"It couldn't have been Mr. Bone," she said.

"Why not?" I asked.

"Because," Rose said slowly, "Mr. Bone answered the phone when I called Nicholas at the funeral home."

We stared at each other.

"How is that even possible?" Poppy said.

"Maybe we were wrong," I said. "Maybe whoever it was just resembled Mr. Bone."

"You're kidding, right?" Poppy said. "That guy was the spitting image of Mr. Bone."

"Well, he can't be in two places at once, can he?" I challenged, but Poppy didn't have an answer.

"Where'd Mr. Bone the Second go?" Poppy said.

"He just disappeared," Rose replied. "He was here one minute and then, *poof!*"

We exchanged glances. "He was acting really spacey," I said.

Poppy said slowly, "And he's not the only one."

"If I didn't know any better, I'd say Mr. Bone has a clone, just like in one of those science fiction movies," I joked.

Rose glared at me. "Don't even joke about that."

"What?" I was startled by my normally placid sister's temper.

"About clones," she said. "Human cloning is a very controversial issue. There's no way someone at campus would clone a human being."

I frowned at her, perplexed. "No one said anything about anyone on campus creating a clone. Besides, I was just joking."

Why was she so touchy?

"I'm sorry, Daisy. I'm a little sensitive. Some people have criticized Dr. Franken about her research methods."

"What are you trying to say? That Dr. Franken is involved in cloning?"

"Of course not," she said hotly.

Rose definitely had some hero worship thing going on with Dr. Franken. I couldn't imagine why, because from what I could see, the doctor didn't treat my sister very well.

"I'm trying to say that there's something weird going on in Nightshade. Weirder than usual," she said. "And the Nightshade City Council wants our help finding out what that weirdness is."

An actual invitation to a council meeting? I was thrilled.

CHAPTER TWELVE

The Nightshade City Council meetings were usually held at Mort's Mortuary, the funeral home Mr. Bone owned, but this time the meeting was up at the Wilder Mansion, that historic home of Elise Wilder and her grandmother. There was an elegant restaurant on the premises, and a large ballroom where the city council would be meeting. It was also where we had had our prom—the last place Poppy had seen Gage.

Five minutes before midnight, my sisters and I stood on the doorstep of the mansion and knocked on the huge, ornately carved wooden door. It creaked open, and we were greeted by a petite woman with long black hair, piercing eyes, and a slinky black dress.

"Bianca!" I said, surprised. "It's great to see you. How are you?" She was a shifter who had once saved my life, when she was in feline form. Who says black cats are unlucky? I hadn't realized she was still in town. Then again, I didn't get up to the restaurant in the mansion, where she worked, all that often.

Cheeseburgers were more my speed than Cornish game hen. Although I would like to learn how to prepare that dish one day.

"I'm fine, Daisy," Bianca said, leading us down the hall toward the ballroom. "We're glad you could make it to the meeting."

"We're thrilled to be invited," I said.

"The council doesn't seem to be so secret anymore," Poppy commented. The Nightshade City Council meetings were usually confined to the original thirteen families, though I had managed to sneak into one once.

A troubled look crossed Bianca's face in the candlelight flickering from golden sconces on the walls. "These are extraordinary circumstances and the council thought it best to inform all paranormally connected residents about what's going on," she explained.

"What *is* going on?" Poppy asked anxiously.

"Patience, Poppy," Rose said sharply. She obviously didn't want to break any council protocol.

The Wilders were one of Nightshade's original thirteen families. Portraits of their stern-looking ancestors lined the walls of the hall. I was looking at one of a wide-eyed woman in a high-necked blouse. When I glanced back again, she had transformed into an owl. When I looked again, she was merely a woman with a hooked nose, round eyes, and snowy hair.

Bianca heard my gasp of surprise and smiled knowingly. "There's a long legacy of shifters in Nightshade," she said.

That reminded me that Bianca was good friends with a certain shifter family who I had some questions about. "How are the Paxtons these days?" I asked.

Bianca sighed. "Not so good," she said. "Their youngest son is not adjusting well to his change. Apparently they couldn't even get him to calm down enough to come to the meeting tonight. All new werewolves go through some difficult times, of course, but Wolfgang seems to be having an especially rough go of it."

"Do you think he's acting up just because he's a new shifter, or is there something more to it?" I asked.

"I don't know, Daisy," Bianca admitted. "All I know is that his parents are at the end of their rope."

We had reached the ballroom. I could hear the rumbling of voices on the other side of the doors.

"Is it going to be hard for you to go in there?" Rose asked, putting a comforting hand on Poppy's shoulder.

"Of course not," Poppy said. "It's where Gage first told me he loved me. Besides, I can't wait to hear what the council has to say." With that, she bravely opened the door and led us into the room.

When I saw the size of the crowd in the ballroom, I realized why this meeting wasn't being held at Mort's. There was no way the Tranquility Room would hold this many people.

I recognized quite a few of my classmates and former classmates. Elise Wilder and Bane Paxton were there, although not in Were form. They were holding hands and ignoring everyone around them.

I don't know how I ever suspected Elise of being interested in Ryan. From the way she was looking at Bane, she was clearly into him.

I spotted Ryan sitting a couple of rows from the front. He motioned for us to join him. I saw there were open chairs next to his.

"There's Ryan," I said to Poppy. "Let's go sit by him."

She followed me through the crowd. Rose had already made a beeline for Nicholas, who was lurking in a corner.

"Welcome back!" I said happily.

"Hi there," Ryan said as I slid into the seat next to him and Poppy grabbed the seat next to me. "Dad drove nonstop to get back in time for the meeting."

"I stopped at Slim's for coffee," he said, handing a cup to each of us.

Mine was a vanilla latte, just the way I liked it.

"You're the best," I said. I gave him a quick kiss.

He grinned at me. "Coffee is the only way I'll make it through tonight. I can't get used to these midnight meetings," he explained. "I've skipped most of them lately, but Nicholas called me today and said it was important that I attend. Does either of you know what's up?"

I started to answer but was interrupted by Natalie. "Daisy,

do you mind if we sit by you? Grandma's not feeling very well and most of the chairs are already taken."

"Of course, go ahead and take these," I said, moving back so they could get through the aisle.

Natalie helped her grandma sit down. Mrs. Mason didn't look very well at all. She was wearing a hot-pink tracksuit and bright white running shoes, but her face was gray.

"So, how's your grandmother?" I asked Ryan.

"Her hip has mended completely," he said. "She's as good as new."

"Already?"

"It's the Were blood," he explained.

"Your grandma is a werewolf, too?" I hadn't really thought about who else in Ryan's family had the trait.

"Yes," he confirmed, then laughed at my expression. "But relax. The scariest thing she does is make T-shirts covered in metallic buttons."

"What does she think of you dating a non-Were?"

He shrugged. "It never came up. But it's not a big deal. My mom is a norm, too."

Ryan never talked about his mom. She'd left Ryan and his dad years ago and now lived in San Francisco with her new boyfriend.

I shot him a curious look. "Does she know about . . . ?"

"About me being a werewolf? Yes."

I wanted to ask him if he'd told Sean yet, but our conversation was cut off when a gavel sounded from the front of the room. Mr. Bone stood at the podium, in a long black robe, calling, "Order!" over the rumbling of the crowd. Most people there wouldn't recognize that the leader of the Nightshade City Council was one and the same as the round, perpetually sunburned golf-loving funeral home owner we called Mort. The creature there at the podium had a skull for a face.

Nicholas was adopted, which explained why he hadn't inherited the same paranormal trait as his father. I'd met many paranormals in the last few months, but I'd never met another Skull.

When the room finally quieted down, Skull, AKA Mr. Bone, said, "Thank you all for coming. A grave matter has come to my attention. After several reports of strange behavior by various Nightshade residents, the council has determined that our town is plagued by doppelgangers."

The room burst into loud conversation. Everyone talked at once as Mr. Bone banged on his gavel. No one paid attention. I could tell what he was saying had some sort of significance for many of the older city council members, but I had no idea what was going on.

An elderly Were stood up and yelled over the din, "But there hasn't been any word of doppelgangers in almost fifty years. You're telling us that they've returned and have descended upon Nightshade?"

"What's a doppelganger?" I whispered to Ryan and Poppy.

A droopy-looking harpy in the row behind us overheard me. "A doppelganger is an exact double. A very dangerous double."

"You mean like an evil twin or something?"

"Exactly," she replied. "And if the real person should ever meet his double . . ." She shuddered.

"What? What will happen?" Poppy said. I knew she was wondering if the man I'd seen outside Slim's was really our father or just some sort of DoppelDad.

"If you come face-to-face with your doppelganger, legend has it that you will die."

Skull gave up banging on his gavel and began shouting, "Quiet, please. Please, there's no need to panic. We must have order."

"Why is everyone so upset?" I asked Ryan, but Mr. Bone's next words answered my question.

"Doppelgangers love to create chaos and we cannot allow that to happen!"

"Where did they come from?" asked one of the vampires. She looked familiar and I realized I had seen her at the very first city council meeting I had attended, although that one had been without an invitation.

"We don't know," Skull admitted. "There is a suspicion that someone, maybe even someone in Nightshade, is creating new doppelgangers, using simple material, like a piece of the person's hair, and magic. We plan to . . . address this, but our number one priority now is to get rid of them before they take over the lives of our residents."

I shivered. That sounded sinister.

Mrs. Mason gave a little moan, and when I looked at her, her hands were trembling as if she was nervous.

"If they're exact doubles, how are we supposed to know who's a doppelganger and who's just a regular person?" I wondered aloud.

"I have a feeling we're about to find out," said Ryan.

Chief Mendez stood and said, "We believe they're in town to discredit our citizens. Doppelgangers will deliberately destroy someone's life. They behave horribly, make mischief, and then watch as the person they resemble has their life ruined."

After his pronouncement, he left the room and then returned, wheeling a large cage with golden bars. Inside was none other than Miss McBennett from the post office. The crowd gasped.

"This is not really Miss McBennett," Skull assured the crowd.

Nevertheless, it was an unsettling sight. The frail-looking woman inside the cage shook the bars angrily. When Chief Mendez wheeled her past the refreshment table in the corner of the ballroom, she reached out in a desperate attempt to swipe a cookie. She snarled when the cookie remained out of reach.

I leaned into Ryan. "That's some sweet tooth," I said softly.

The harpy heard me. "Sugar," she said in a gloomy voice. "There are doppelgangers in Nightshade, definitely. They can't get enough sugar. You see someone with a vacant look in his eye and stuffing his face full of sugar, you'd better believe it's a doppelganger."

A moment later Skull confirmed what the harpy said. "Be on the lookout for anyone who consumes an unusually large amount of sugar."

The woman in the cage let out a feeble moan. "Why have you brought me here, Chief Mendez? Why, I've known you since you were a boy."

For a minute, she had everyone convinced she was the real Miss McBennett. A vampire even jumped to his feet and said, "Let the poor old woman go." The crowd broke into noisy debate.

Chief Mendez held up a hand for quiet and then when the noise finally died down, said, "The real Miss McBennett is here. Miss McBennett, please come forward."

A woman stepped out of the shadows and walked up to the cage.

"You can't tell the difference, can you?" the chief continued.

"Doppelgangers have knowledge of the memories and experiences of their double," Skull explained. "This makes them very convincing."

The crowd shifted in their seats uncomfortably. What was going to happen? Clearly, the legend about dying if you came face-to-face with your double must only be a myth because both Miss McBennetts in the front of the room were alive and well.

"I don't even want to know why the Wilders have that cage in their house," I muttered to Poppy.

She giggled and unwrapped a piece of gum. She always chewed gum when she was nervous.

Suddenly the woman in the cage went wild. "I smell sugar!" she cried, looking straight at Poppy.

Poppy gave a little yelp and quickly popped the gum into her mouth.

The doppelganger threw herself against the cage, screaming hoarsely and rattling the bars. In the next few minutes, she begged, pleaded, and threatened, all for a little bit of sugar.

After he thought that the point had been sufficiently made, Mr. Bone tossed a couple of cookies into the cage and the doppelganger gobbled them down frantically.

Clearly, the demonstration proved that the doppelganger was the one who was caged.

Even though my brain told me that it wasn't really Miss McBennett, it gave me the shivers.

The real Miss McBennett was led away to a seat far from her mirror image. Finally, her double's hunger seemed to subside. "May I have a little more, please?" she said in a sweet voice.

"First tell us who made you," Mr. Bone said.

A sly look crossed her face. "What will you give me?"

Mr. Bone waved a whole pie in front of her. A greedy look

came over her face, and she seemed to consider it. After a moment, though, she shook her head, then cackled. "By the time you figure it out, it'll be too late."

Mr. Bone gave her the pie, anyway. Most of the audience turned away. It wasn't a pretty sight to see an eighty-year-old woman gulping down fistfuls of pie with her bare hands.

"We just wave sugar in front of them?" Bane said doubtfully.

"Yes," Skull responded. "It's that simple. But we've got to capture them first—and keep them from sugar for a few hours. They'll go wild trying to get to it."

"If you see a doppelganger, report it immediately to me at the Nightshade police department," Chief Mendez said. "Or tell any other council member and we'll take care of it right away."

I squirmed in my seat and glanced at Ryan. I hadn't told him yet about seeing my dad. Or maybe it was just a doppelganger. I wanted to wait until I knew for sure before reporting him to the city council.

After the meeting was over, Rose left with Nicholas. As Ryan walked Poppy and me to the car, Poppy tactfully strode ahead of us.

Ryan took my hand. "Promise me you'll be careful?" he said. "Don't go meeting your double in a dark alley."

"I promise." I hesitated.

I don't know why I was reluctant to mention it to Ryan, especially after everything we'd already been through. If I couldn't trust him by now, when would I?

I took a deep breath. "Speaking of doubles," I said, "you'll never guess who I saw hanging out by Slim's dumpster . . ."

After I'd let it all spill out, there was silence. I stole a peek at Ryan. He looked lost in thought.

"So what do you think it all means?" I asked.

"I have no idea," Ryan admitted. "But since doppelgangers are doubles of living people, it does mean one thing for sure. It's possible that your dad—your real dad, not the imitation—is still alive."

"Do you really think so?" I was afraid to hope.

Ryan looked doubtful. "I don't know, Daisy," he said. "If you see this guy again, please call me or my dad. The council can find out for sure if it's your real dad or just a doppelganger."

"You have a point," I admitted. Now was not the time to throw caution to the wind, no matter how much I wanted it to really be my dad.

I kissed Ryan good night and assured him again I'd call him if I saw the mysterious man. But in my heart, I wasn't sure *what* I would do if I saw my dad again.

CHAPTER THIRTEEN

I had the early shift at Slim's the next day, which meant I should have gone to sleep immediately after the meeting. Instead, I lay awake thinking about what Ryan had said. Was it possible that my father was alive and well? Then, why hadn't he contacted us?

I must have finally fallen asleep, because I jerked awake when the alarm rang. I'd been having a marvelous dream, in which the entire Giordano family was reunited with my father.

I made it to Slim's on autopilot. Though I was barely awake, I managed to notice Flo's T-shirt, which read I AM THE EVIL TWIN.

Despite an extra-large latte, I was practically sleepwalking through the lunch rush.

Even Slim noticed. "Daisy, are you all right?"

I smothered a yawn. "Why do you ask?"

"Because you just put nuts in that salad. Mr. Webster ordered it without. He's allergic."

"Oh, my gosh!" I set the salad aside and started a new one. "It'll take me just a minute."

"It's okay," he said. A spatula pointed me toward the front. "Get yourself a cup of coffee. I can handle it for a bit."

I grabbed the largest coffee cup I could find and headed for the pot. My back was turned away from the door, but I heard it open and then Flo's gasp.

"Daisy, is that you?" There was something familiar about the voice. I turned as a tall dark-haired man in a suit approached the counter. I suppressed a gasp of my own. My father's face stared back at me. "Can I help you?"

"It's me, your father. Don't you recognize me?"

The jukebox kicked on. The song playing was "Lips Like Sugar" by Echo and the Bunnymen. Coincidence? I remembered the harpy had said that doppelgangers loved sugar.

Lil was definitely trying to tell me something. "How do I know you're my father?" I asked. He didn't look like the desperate guy who had been dumpster diving the other day. He was clean and well-dressed.

"The first thing you ever cooked was pancakes. And you burned them."

But he had eaten every bite, I remembered, and then taught me how to use the stove properly. I relaxed a little. I figured he would, too, if I got him some refreshments.

"Can I get you something?" Test number one.

"Black coffee, please."

"Would you like a donut with that?"

His eyes jittered to the display case, but his expression remained serene. "No, thanks. Just the coffee, please."

I bent under the counter, where we kept our coffee cups, and caught a whiff of his cologne. It sent a pang through me. It was a smell I'd never forget. Dreamer by Versace. Dad had worn it as long as I could remember.

I set the cup in front of him and poured it, then scooted the sugar container closer to him. He passed that test, too, when he carefully chose three packets of sugar and stirred them into his coffee. A tiny bloom of hope grew in my chest. That was exactly how my dad used to take his coffee. He used to let me put the sugar cubes in his cup for him when I was little.

"Where have you been? Why haven't you been in contact with us?"

"My memory is fuzzy," he replied. "I'm not sure exactly what happened. I guess I must have been unconscious . . . And when I woke up, I was being dumped out of a van onto the beach here in Nightshade. I don't remember where I was or who I was with before that. I was so confused. I slept under the boardwalk and ate out of dumpsters for days. It took me awhile, but I started to regain memories of my life in Nightshade. But there are still big gaps."

Amnesia? Or maybe his faulty memory was just a cover.

Before I had time to think about it, I was in his mind. I caught a glimpse of a tiny room without windows and a voice saying, "I'm not done with you yet." The memories whirled through my consciousness. He was knocked on the head and abducted. I jumped out of his mind when I started delving into his memories of when I was a kid. It hurt too much to remember how happy we were then.

His voice interrupted my rummaging in his memories. "You've grown up. I barely recognized you," he said. I wondered if he knew I had psychic powers. I doubted it. When I last saw him, I hadn't had any abilities.

I certainly didn't look the same as I did when I was twelve. But to me, he looked like the same old dad.

But if he remembered where he was held captive, why was he pretending he didn't?

Without thinking, I snapped, "It's not like the world stopped when you went away." I felt a pang of regret immediately after saying it. My long-standing bitterness about his absence was slipping out.

"No, of course not," he said softly. "How is your mother?"

"Why haven't you called her to tell her you're back? She's never changed her cell phone number." She didn't want to, just in case he somehow decided to contact her.

I realized that I was talking much too loudly when I saw

Flo's face. She grabbed a rag and began wiping down the stainless steel, but I knew she was listening to every word.

He shrugged. "I told you, there are gaps in my memory. I don't remember her number. And besides, I heard she was in Italy for the summer. I'd rather just wait until she gets home so we can talk in person."

"But she's your wife," I said, trying to keep my voice down. To my amazement, he wasn't paying attention to me. He was staring at the clock behind me above the wall.

"Am I keeping you from something?" I said sarcastically.

"No, it's just, this isn't the place for this discussion. We'll talk later, at home." He carefully adjusted his wristwatch and, before I could speak, threw a bill on the counter and walked out.

Unbelievable.

"Was that your father?" Flo's voice broke into my thoughts.

"Apparently." But I wasn't sure. My memories of my father had faded over time. *Wait—he said we'd talk at home? I really* needed to talk to Poppy and Rose.

I kept getting Rose's voice mail but reached Poppy and gave her a brief summary of the conversation I'd just had.

Poppy was supposed to pick me up after work, so we decided we'd head to the university after that. Rose was bound to be there; she'd been spending every extra minute at the lab lately.

I went back to the kitchen. The orders had backed up a little while I'd been chatting with . . . who exactly? I thought about the identity of the person calling himself my father while I helped Slim cook, but I didn't find any answers.

After my shift finally ended, I told Poppy all about what had happened.

"Why didn't you make him wait until I could get there?" she asked.

"He took me by surprise. I wasn't expecting him to stroll into Slim's, you know. I'm not even sure it *was* Dad, especially not with all those doppelgangers running around town."

"What if it is?"

"Let's find Rose first. Then we'll figure out what to do."

When we got to the lab, it was locked up tight, but I could hear raised voices on the other side of the door. It sounded like they were arguing about something.

The knob turned and I stepped back as Mrs. Mason stormed out, with Dr. Franken at her heels.

"Come back here, Matilda!" Dr. Franken shouted, but Mrs. Mason ignored her and hurried down the hall and out of sight.

The professor's expression was unreadable, but I noticed that her hands clenched and unclenched rapidly. She didn't even notice us until Poppy peered into the lab's open doorway.

"Stay away from there," Dr. Franken said sharply. Then she recognized us and added, "Oh, I'm sorry. It's just that there's highly sensitive research in the lab. You're Rose's sisters, correct?"

"Yes, we'd like to speak to her if it's at all possible," Poppy said in a quietly respectful tone.

"Wait here, I'll go get Rose," she replied, then entered the lab and closed the door firmly behind her.

We cooled our heels in the hallway until Rose finally appeared, wearing her white lab coat.

"Is everything okay?" she asked.

"We need to talk to you. Privately."

"Daisy, I'm in the middle of something big. Can't it wait?"

"It's important," Poppy replied. "Really. But we can't talk here." I glanced at her. Was she as creeped out as I was by Dr. Franken?

Rose looked at her watch. "Meet me at the food court in half an hour."

"Rose, Rose?" Dr. Franken's voice called out. "Where is that girl?"

"I've got to get back," Rose said. "Half an hour." She didn't wait for an answer, but strode back into the lab without a backward glance.

Poppy and I walked to the student center. There were quite a few more people on campus today, including, evidently, good-looking frat boys. Poppy guy-watched appreciatively.

When we got to the food court, I ordered an extra-large vanilla latte for me and sodas for Poppy and Rose.

Rose rushed in about forty-five minutes later, after Poppy had managed to finish her soda and order another one, plus an order of onion rings.

"I can only stay for a minute," Rose said. "Something set Dr. Franken off this morning and she's in a tizzy. I don't dare stay too long." She grabbed an onion ring. "I'm starving. I didn't have time for lunch today."

She looked from Poppy to me expectantly.

There was no good way to break the news. "Dad's in town," I said. "I had a visit from him at Slim's today."

Rose's mouth dropped open. "You mean it's really him?"

"I don't know," I admitted. "But I think he's going to move in. He said he'd see me at the house later."

Rose looked at her watch. "I know Dr. Franken needs me, but I can't let you two go back there alone," she said. "I'll just have to call her and tell her I had a family emergency and I need to take off the rest of the day."

"Do you think it could really be Dad?" Poppy asked after Rose made her call. There was a tiny bit of hope in Poppy's voice.

"It could be, but we should wait to tell Mom until we're sure. There's no sense in getting her all upset if it turns out it's not even him."

"So what should we do in the meantime?" I asked as we hurried to the car.

"We'll go home and entertain him, whoever he is," Rose said. "And we'll try to find out who he really is. We can't get too close to him before we know for sure."

"This feels wrong," Poppy said. "If he's our dad, we should be welcoming him home with open arms."

Rose thought for a moment. "We'll tell him that we need time to reacquaint ourselves with him. Break it to him gently."

But it turned out we didn't have to worry about the right way to tell him. When we got home, the house was empty. It looked like our father had vanished again.

CHAPTER FOURTEEN

I had to work at Slim's the next day, as well. When I got there, the lights were off and the front door was still locked. Not like Slim at all. If he was going to be late, he always made sure to call me or he asked me ahead of time to cover for him.

I went around to the back door and was alarmed to find that it was wide open. I entered cautiously, but there was no sign of a break-in or any damage. There was also no sign of Slim. It was hard enough to tell if he was around during the best of times, but how exactly did you look for someone you couldn't see?

"Slim?" I called, wondering if this was another test. I quickly dismissed the idea. The ovens were cold and the counters were empty. Slim would never mess with the diner's schedule, and as my watch told me, there was less than half an hour before the diner was supposed to open.

I went to the tiny office, found an employee phone list, and dialed Slim's number. There was a pile of candy wrappers on the desk, next to the phone.

I let it ring several times, but Slim didn't pick up. Would it kill him to join the twenty-first century and get an answering machine?

Finally, in desperation, I dialed Flo's cell.

"What?" Flo sounded cranky and I couldn't blame her. She wasn't due in for hours.

"It's Daisy. Sorry to wake you, but Slim's not at the diner this morning and nothing's been prepped. I can handle the kitchen, but I'm worried about him."

She sighed. "I'll be right in. And Daisy, don't worry about him. I'm sure he's just fine." There was an edge in her voice. She hung up without saying goodbye, but I couldn't really blame her. She'd worked the late shift the night before. What was going on with Slim? And why wasn't Flo more worried about him?

I didn't have time to analyze the situation. The restaurant had to open.

I hurried back to the kitchen and examined the specials board. There wasn't enough time to prepare the vegetable quiche Slim had planned. I wiped the board clean and printed VEGE-TABLE OMELET under SPECIALS.

Our regulars would start a riot if we didn't serve Slim's melt-in-your-mouth cinnamon rolls. I fired up the oven and crossed my fingers that we had enough dough.

When I went to the refrigerator to check, it was wide open, and food containers were strewn all over the floor, including the pan with today's cinnamon rolls. There were only a few globs of dough left on it.

I had barely processed what the mess meant, when in the next room, the jukebox sprang to life, blasting the Archies' "Sugar, Sugar." My heart began to pound. Was someone in the restaurant?

I grabbed a knife and crept to the dining room, staying low, to hide behind the counter. Despite the loud music, I could hear a rustling at the end of the counter. I crouched lower and squeezed into a little nook beside the icemaker, where I wouldn't be seen during what I was sure must be a robbery in progress.

From where I crouched, I could see the lower half of the intruder's body. He looked like a big guy. His shoes looked familiar. His pants, too. Ryan's dad always wore shoes and pants like that. Those were cop clothes.

Feeling a little safer, I edged out of my hiding place and stood up. I was shocked to see Deputy Denton single-handedly consuming all the goodies in Slim's rotating dessert display case.

He saw me and dropped a gloopy handful of lemon meringue pie. He tried to speak but his mouth was full. I knew right away that I'd have to use a different kind of weapon against this intruder.

Luckily, the police station was right across the street. I grabbed a sugar shaker from the counter and approached the Deputy Denton look-alike, brandishing the sugar in front of him. He stared at it as if hypnotized.

I poured the sugar on the floor and moved backward toward the door. Deputy Doppelganger followed the trail, only pausing to grab a handful of mints from the bowl next to the cash register on his way out.

I kept the sugar trail going across the street, which, fortunately, was not busy at that early hour. When we entered the police station, Chief Mendez looked up from his desk.

"Daisy? Deputy Denton?" he said, looking confused.

"That isn't Deputy Denton," I said, holding up the sugar shaker. "It's a doppelganger."

The chief moved to grab the doppelganger before he could get away. "I knew there was something wrong when Deputy Denton came into work so early this morning and took the master keys."

I blushed. I knew the keys the chief was talking about. They opened every door in town, and Ryan and I had used them a few times to get into places we weren't supposed to be. That explained how Deputy Doppelganger had gotten into Slim's.

Chief Mendez plucked the keys out of the offender's pocket and led him back to the small station's single holding cell.

"Thanks, Daisy," the chief said when the doppelganger was locked up tight. "You did a great job getting him here."

"No problem," I said, then looked at my watch. *Yikes.* "I'd better get back to work."

As I hurried toward the door, I passed the real Deputy Denton on his way in to work. His eyes widened when he saw his double in the holding cell. "What the . . ."

I didn't stop to explain. I had a lot of cleaning up to do at Slim's.

Back at the diner, I scrambled to sweep up the dessert-splattered floor. Luckily, there was some extra dough for cinnamon rolls in the back of the fridge that the doppelganger hadn't discovered, so I quickly prepped the rolls and slid them in to bake. I chopped vegetables for the omelets, then hurried to the front to start a pot of coffee.

I tried to remember what else to do to prepare for the breakfast rush, but my mind was blank. Slim was usually there to walk me through it.

I checked my watch again. When was Flo going to get here? I cringed when I saw a line of customers outside the front door already waiting for the restaurant to open.

It was like a bad dream. All I needed now was for Wolfgang and the football team or the cheerleaders to show up and my day would be complete.

I checked the clock over the cash register. There was no help for it; it was time to open. To my surprise, Mrs. Mason, Natalie's grandmother, was first in line.

"Quit dilly-dallying, girl, and get me some coffee," she barked as I unlocked the door and turned the sign to OPEN.

"It-it's not ready yet," I stuttered.

"Why not? Young people have no sense of responsibility these days."

"Ease up on Daisy, Mrs. Mason," Flo said, as she slipped inside, behind the older woman. "Slim didn't show up this morning."

Mrs. Mason didn't answer, but I noticed her chilly expression thawed a bit. "Is my granddaughter here this morning?"

"Not yet," Flo answered, "but I expect she'll meet Slim for breakfast."

As if on cue, Natalie strolled in and gave everyone a bright smile. "Good morning, everyone." But then she spotted her grandmother and her spine slumped. "Grandmother, what are you doing here?"

"Is that any way to greet your own flesh and blood?" Mrs. Mason replied. "I came here to speak to you, since you do not have the decency to return my calls."

"I thought Natalie lived with her grandma," I whispered to Flo.

"They had a fight, so she's been spending a lot of time with Slim," Flo replied.

Mrs. Mason said, "I'd like a cinnamon roll when you two are done gossiping."

"The cinnamon rolls aren't done yet," I told Flo. "What are we going to do?"

"Improvise," she said. And that's exactly what we did. I managed to keep Mrs. Mason happy by promising her a free cinnamon roll, once they came out of the oven.

About an hour later, I was in the kitchen, taking out the second batch of rolls, when I heard the back door open, and then Slim's cheerful whistling filled the kitchen.

"Daisy, you're a lifesaver," he said. "Could I trouble you for a cup of coffee from the front?"

I nearly dropped the pan. "Sure, Slim."

"I'll frost the rolls while you do that. Extra cream, please."

I hurried to the front, where Flo was manning the cash register.

"He's here," I said. "And he's *whistling*." Slim was not a whistler.

"Did he say anything?" she asked me as she handed change to the customer. We kept our eyes focused on his back as he exited the restaurant, but I knew we were both dying to stare in the direction of the kitchen. Invisible man or not, my curiosity was killing me. Where had Slim been and why was he so cheerful?

"Just thanks and that he'd like a cup of coffee."

"Slim's back?" That from Natalie.

Flo and I exchanged glances. Not to be shallow, but dating an invisible man was bound to be complicated. I waited until Natalie was out of earshot.

"What's going on with Slim?"

"He's doing some undercover work for the council. It must be going well, because he's in a better mood than I've seen him all month."

"Deep undercover, obviously." I giggled.

"Something about the doppelgangers," Flo said quietly, after a quick glance at Mrs. Mason, who seemed absorbed in her breakfast. "That's all I know. He's being secretive." She slammed the cash register drawer shut.

I paused. "I think someone may be on to him," I whispered. Then I told her about discovering Deputy Doppelganger in the diner earlier that morning.

"Maybe he just wanted some pie," Flo replied, eying the empty dessert display case.

"Maybe," I said. "But things looked out of place in the office and there were candy wrappers all over Slim's desk."

She frowned. "It's probably nothing," she finally said, "but you should mention it to Slim, just in case. But not in front of Natalie."

"Okay. I'd better get back there." I grabbed a couple of mugs and filled them with coffee before hurrying back to the kitchen.

I handed Slim his cup, then remembered. "I forgot your cream."

"Don't worry about it, Daisy. There's milk in the walk-in."

I remembered Flo's advice and gave Slim a quick rundown of what I'd observed that morning. I was too busy to dwell on Slim's extracurricular activities any longer, but I did notice that throughout the morning, nothing got to him. Not when I overcooked Mr. Bone's steak and scrambled instead of fried his eggs, not when Flo broke a half-dozen plates, and not even when the dishwasher called in sick. Slim just kept whistling.

It was kind of annoying, actually, especially when Natalie kept shooting him lovesick looks when she thought no one was watching.

After my shift was over, I found a message on my cell from Rose, telling me to hurry home.

When I walked into the living room, Grandma Giordano was there. My grandma was tall and thin, with deep-set brown eyes. Her hair was a gorgeous shade of silver and she wore a pair of trousers, which fit her perfectly, and a cream silk blouse. I'd never seen my grandma in a pair of shorts, even on the hottest day.

Her gaze focused on the door behind me. "Where is he?"

My sisters and I exchanged glances.

"He's . . ." I hesitated.

"Did you think my own son wouldn't call me? I've already heard the news. It's all over town. Where is he?"

"Grandma," Poppy said, "we're not sure it's Dad."

"Of course it is. Do you think I wouldn't remember my own son?"

Our cautious, rational grandmother had completely lost it. I took a deep breath. "You had to have heard about the doppel-gangers?"

"Yes, but what does that have to do with your father?" I

recognized that stubborn look. It was the same one I'd get on my face occasionally.

"Maybe nothing, but we want to be sure it was him. Something seemed off when he visited me at Slim's."

"Off how?" Grandma sounded defensive.

"Why hasn't he contacted Mom?"

"Your mother is in Italy. He wants to talk to her face-to-face. Wouldn't you?"

She had a point. My memories of my dad had faded. And I didn't have the heart to extinguish that hopeful light in her eye. Evidently, neither did Poppy or Rose.

A key turned in the door, and a second later, Dad strode into the room. "Girls, I'm home!" he said cheerily.

A key chain with WORLD'S GREATEST DAD on it dangled from his hand. I gasped. I remembered giving him one just like that for Father's Day when I was nine.

"Poppy," he said. "You've cut your hair." When my father left, Poppy still had hair down to her waist.

That stopped her in her tracks, but she recovered swiftly. "That long hair was a pain to take care of, Dad."

I could see that Poppy's resolve to keep Dad at arm's length until we were sure about his identity was fading fast. "Oh, Daddy, I'm so glad you're back," she cried, and rushed toward him. He embraced her in a rather stiff-looking hug.

As he hugged my sister, I studied his face carefully. He'd always been handsome, but age had added distinction to his good looks.

"And Rose," he said when Poppy finally let go of him, "I can't believe how you've grown. You're a woman now."

Rose shifted uncomfortably and mumbled a hello.

"Rafe, it's been so long," Grandma said.

"I know, Mama, and I'm sorry," he said. He embraced her, and I could see tears in Grandma's eyes.

"We have a lot of catching up to do," Dad said. "Do you mind if we go outside? Confined spaces make me nervous."

"Of course," Grandma Giordano said. "You poor thing. Locked up all that time." The two of them strode arm in arm out to the backyard.

I rolled my eyes. You could hardly call our spacious living room "confined."

After they were out of earshot, Rose said in a low voice, "What are we going to do?"

"There's nothing we can do, not as long as we don't know for sure who this guy is."

"What if he is Dad?"

"It's possible," I said.

"He had a key, Daisy," Poppy pointed out. "And it worked. He even had the same key chain as Dad. If it's not him, how do you explain that?"

I shrugged. "I don't know, but the timing is suspect."

"Not necessarily," Poppy replied. "Maybe there's a reason he hasn't shown up until now. Like, he didn't know what kind of reception he'd get. He has no way of knowing that Mom has been—"

"Pining for him? True, but I don't think we should say anything to her when she calls."

"What if he answers the phone?"

"We'll have to make sure that doesn't happen," Rose said. "Just until we can investigate him."

Poppy looked appalled. "Investigate our own father?"

"Investigate the man who *might be* our father," I said. "He could be a DoppelDad, remember? He said he doesn't recall how he was abducted, but I read his mind and found out that he *does* have memories of it. Why would he keep that knowledge from us?"

"Maybe to protect us," Poppy said.

"We can't just walk up to him and start asking questions," Rose said. "If he's a phony, he's not just going to confess to it."

"True," I replied. "But it's natural that we'd be curious about where he's been."

"We need to look for a sign that he's a fake," Rose said.

"Like what?" Poppy asked.

"Sugar," I said. "Remember, at the council meeting they said that doppelgangers love sugar."

"Dad has a sweet tooth," Rose pointed out. "That's going to make it tougher to figure out if this guy's real or not."

"I don't remember that," I said stubbornly.

"Well, he used to, anyway," she replied, with a shrug. "People do change, but don't you remember how Mom would always buy him chocolate from that little place on the boardwalk? He loved chocolate, just like you."

I hadn't remembered, not until now. What else had I forgotten in the years since I'd seen my father?

"We should concentrate on finding out more about him," I said. "Grandma's keeping him occupied for now, but I'll try to keep an eye on him and see if he lets anything slip."

"You're the youngest. Why do you get Dad?" Poppy asked.

"Because I'm the one he approached. That means he thinks I'm the weakest link."

"Or maybe it really is Dad and he just missed you."

"We can't think that way, not yet." *Not even as much as I want to think that way.* "Not until we have proof that he could be our father."

Just then there was a knock on the door. I looked at my watch. "Oh no," I said. "It's probably Ryan. We have a date tonight."

"Obviously, you can't go now," Poppy said, nodding in the direction of Dad.

"Tell him you're sick," Rose said.

"I don't like lying to my boyfriend," I protested.

"It's a white lie," Rose said softly. "If Ryan finds out Dad is here, he'll tell his dad, who will tell the whole council, who will come over here and take him away to see if he's a doppelganger. I think we should try to see if we can figure this out on our own first, don't you?"

I nodded, recalling how upset Deputy Doppelganger had looked in the holding cell this morning. I didn't want my dad—if he was—to be there unless it was absolutely necessary. Finally I answered the door, only opening it a crack.

"Hey," Ryan said hesitantly when he saw me still wearing my food-splattered apron from work. "Are you okay? Did you forget we have plans tonight?"

"No, I was going to call you. I'm not feeling too well. I think I'm just going to relax at home tonight."

"Oh," Ryan said. "Well, do you need some company? Can I come in?"

"You'd better not," I said. "I wouldn't want you to catch anything. So . . . I'll call you when I feel better, okay?"

Ryan stuck his foot in the door to prevent me from closing it. "Is there something wrong, Daisy?"

My face flushed bright red. I was a terrible liar. "No, I told you, I'm just sick."

Ryan's eyes narrowed. "This wouldn't happen to have anything to do with your dad, would it? My dad told me that he—or his doppelganger—was spotted in town today. He's not *here*, is he?"

I glanced back at the couch, where Poppy and Rose were shaking their heads and mouthing *no, no, no*.

"No, of course not," I said to Ryan.

I was glad that Dad was still out in the backyard with Grandma, where Ryan couldn't hear or see him.

"Well . . . okay," Ryan said reluctantly. "You will call me or my dad if you see the guy, right?"

I nodded, and faked a few coughs for good measure.

"Get some rest," he said, then leaned over to kiss my forehead.

When I shut the door, Poppy cried, "That was close!"

I hated lying to Ryan. "Now I really do feel sick."

CHAPTER FIFTEEN

The next morning, over a breakfast of strawberry waffles, which I cooked, Dad made the suggestion that Grandma Giordano stay with us during the "adjustment phase."

"I've been gone a long time," he said. "I'm practically a stranger to you all. And I'll need a hand in the kitchen."

Grandma Giordano snorted. "Rafe, you know as well as I do that you're a better cook than I am. And Daisy takes after you. She does most of the cooking, anyway."

"Yes, well, I'm a little rusty in the kitchen," he said. "I was held against my will for so long."

"Held where?" Poppy chimed in.

"I don't know," he replied. He shuddered and a strange look came into his eyes. "It was cold and dark, but there were trees and shrubs all around me."

Rose and I exchanged glances. Dad had disappeared while he was doing research in some forest. The description fit. Maybe we did have our father back.

———

After just a few days, we'd already started to get into a rhythm. Dad would get up early and run to the Donut Hole for a box of donuts. We'd read the paper together, take long walks, and watch television. He laughed insanely at episodes of *The Simpsons*, but he'd always liked that show. He even did a mean Homer impression.

But we hadn't yet cooked a meal together. He'd barely stepped foot in the kitchen. I missed the old days when he'd teach me how to prepare special dishes for the family.

So that morning, I said, "Dad, why don't we make breakfast for the whole family tomorrow? Just you and me, like the old days?" It sounded like I was pleading with him.

"I have a better idea," he said. "Why don't I take you all to breakfast?"

I was disappointed that we wouldn't be spending time in the kitchen, but I nodded in agreement.

When Poppy got up, we all headed to Slim's and found a table in the back. I said hello to a couple of regulars.

Penny Edwards was there, but she ignored me. Her attention was focused on my father. I could practically see the gossip spreading. How would I explain this to Ryan? He still thought I was home sick.

Flo was working, as usual, but to my surprise, Natalie was there helping out. "I was bored waiting for Slim," Natalie announced. "I hope you don't mind that I'm your server."

"Not at all," my father said. "How could I resist such a gorgeous girl?"

Poppy made an *eww* face behind his back. I had to agree with her. Natalie wasn't much older than Rose, and for a minute, it had sounded like Dad was flirting with her. There's nothing more unattractive than some middle-aged guy hitting on a coed.

Or at least that's what *I* thought. But throughout breakfast, my father's attentions to Natalie grew more intense. I squirmed in my seat, but Grandma Giordano seemed oblivious.

"Rafe, what are your plans for the rest of the summer? Are you going to Italy to fetch your wife home?"

I glanced over to gauge Dad's response, but his eyes were firmly planted on Natalie.

Natalie returned with our breakfast. My father leaned in to her as she set down his enormous cinnamon roll, stack of pancakes, and apple juice. "You smell wonderful," he murmured.

Ick! I nudged Rose under the table. She cleared her throat. "Uh, Dad, what are your plans?"

"I wouldn't want to interfere with your mother's work," he finally replied. "Not when there are so many lovely distractions here in Nightshade."

Penny's eyes nearly bulged from her skull and she whipped out her cell phone and started texting quickly.

Things seemed to settle down, at least until it was time to pay the bill. "Mama, I'm afraid I've forgotten my wallet. Could you . . . ?"

124

"Of course," Grandma said, without blinking an eye. She paid the tab and left a healthy tip.

Instead of joining us at the door, Dad stood by the table. When Natalie came by, he reached out and grabbed her around the waist. He said something too low for us to hear, but from the deep blush that appeared on Natalie's face, I was glad I was out of earshot.

She tried to extricate herself, but my father only wrapped her tighter. A minute later, in front of confused onlookers, a KISS THE COOK apron appeared out of nowhere and knocked my father down.

Some of the customers may have been baffled, but I knew it was a very angry Slim. As I helped my father to his feet, I had to repress the urge to knock him down again myself.

Were the rumors true? Was my father a womanizer who had abandoned his wife and children? Was his story of an abduction merely an excuse?

I couldn't deny the fact that he had been going out at night after Poppy, Rose, Grandma, and I had gone to bed. More than once, I was awakened at about two A.M. by the sound of his fumbling footsteps as he made his way upstairs.

Then I had a thought. Our dad may have hidden his true self from his family, but surely his friends knew what he was up to. His closest friend at the time he'd disappeared was also his research partner—Sam's dad.

Maybe it was time to reunite old friends and see if any skeletons tumbled out of the closet. And I didn't mean Skull.

I called Sam that night, to make arrangements for the two of them to meet up.

"Daisy, that's fantastic! You finally have your dad back," she said.

"I'm not sure," I said, and then spent the next half hour hashing over all my fears with her.

"Maybe you're just scared," she said. "After all, even if it wasn't his fault, he did abandon you. I mean, it *felt* like he abandoned you all those years, right?"

"You could be right," I said. "I'll give him a chance."

Before we hung up, I added, "And Sam . . . please don't mention this to Sean. I don't want him telling Ryan."

"What? Why?"

"I just . . . need some time to figure things out," I said.

"Okay." Sam sighed. "My lips are sealed. You two and your secrets."

My mind was too full of thoughts of my dad to interpret that comment. We made plans to meet for coffee at the university that afternoon.

I wandered into the living room. "Dad, would you like to hang out with my friend Samantha and her dad?"

"Do I know her?"

"Yes, Samantha Devereaux and her father." I watched him carefully, but he didn't even flinch when he heard the name. Curious, since Sam's dad had been working on research with my father and had published their findings to great acclaim since his disappearance.

When it was time to go meet Samantha and Mr. Devereaux, I drove, since my dad said his nerves were still shaky from captivity. As we headed to the campus, Dad stared out the car window, turning to get a better look at a woman walking her dog down Main Street.

"Dad!" I groaned.

I was glad there wasn't much eye candy on campus. We were meeting Sam and her father at the food court, and I went to order the coffee while we waited for them. It wasn't long before I saw them coming.

Mr. Devereaux was a distinguished-looking man who many people said looked like George Clooney. All I saw was prematurely gray hair and a nice smile, but whatever.

The small place that he and Sam lived in near the university was a far cry from their former palatial home, but they seemed happier. Sam's mom lived in San Francisco and did occasional fly-by parenting. I don't think Sam had visited her once this summer.

Mr. Devereaux took one look at DoppelDad and nearly fainted. "Rafe?"

"Spenser, how are you?" My heart skipped a beat when Dad called Sam's dad by his first name, but then I realized that if he was a phony, it would have been easy enough to find out Sam's dad's first name by looking it up in the campus directory.

Dad and Mr. Devereaux chatted amiably, but after about an hour, my father stopped trying to hide his boredom. I wanted to smack him for being so rude.

In desperation, Mr. Devereaux turned the conversation to work.

"There have been great strides in cloning in the last few years," he said. "A researcher in San Diego claims to have even cloned humans."

My father looked at his watch. "I'd love to stay and talk shop," he said. "But I have an appointment."

"Let's get together soon," Mr. Devereaux replied.

"I'm not sure that's possible," my dad said. "The ladies, you know." He winked and my stomach curdled. "Now, Daisy, don't look like that. You know your old dad is only joking."

While my dad stood impatiently by the exit, I had a brief word with Sam's dad.

"There is absolutely no way that man is your father," he said. "Not unless he's had a psychotic episode. Your father would never even look at another woman. This man is trying to ruin your father's reputation."

"Why would he do that?"

"I haven't the faintest idea, Daisy, but please be careful," he replied. "And call us if you need anything."

I tried to pretend that the news didn't hurt, and looked

at my watch. "Okay, well thanks for meeting us, anyway," I said. "Maybe I have time to stop by and see Rose at Dr. Franken's lab. She knew Dad, too, so it might be worth getting her opinion."

Mr. Devereaux looked alarmed. "Dr. Franken?"

"Didn't Samantha tell you? My sister Rose is working for her this summer. She was a friend of my father's."

"No," Mr. Devereaux said, "my daughter did not mention that fact to me." He gave Samantha a stern look. Samantha looked confused.

I didn't blame her.

"What's wrong with Dr. Franken?" I asked.

Mr. Devereaux considered how to begin. "I'm not sure what's *wrong* with her," he said delicately, "but she wasn't friends with your father. They were colleagues, but the best description would have been friendly rivals. They certainly weren't close. Your father didn't trust her."

I was surprised by this information. Now I wondered why she would have even hired Rose. My sister was brilliant, but there are juniors and seniors who would kill to work with the doctor. My head was swimming, but all I said was, "Oh. Maybe I shouldn't stop by the lab after all."

Sam swept me into a hug. "He's watching," she said. "So don't react."

I said goodbye and walked back, steeling myself to smile at my fake father.

"That Samantha is quite an attractive young woman, all grown up now."

I looked at him with loathing, realizing I was actually glad he wasn't my real father.

"I remember when the two of you used to play with your dolls. What was her name? Ah, yes, Dolores."

I never played with dolls. I did have a stuffed animal I'd named Dolores.

This man was definitely not my father, but he seemed to have some of my father's memories. Now I was more confused than ever. He didn't seem like the man I used to know, but neither did he seem like a complete stranger. I didn't know what to think. So I pressed him with more questions.

"Have you talked to Mom yet?"

He hesitated, then said, "Not yet."

"Why not?" I know the idea was to keep them apart, but suddenly I was angry all over again on her behalf. "She is your wife, after all."

"It's been a long time, Daisy," he said. "I wasn't sure if she . . ." He looked at his feet.

I tried not to, but I felt a little sorry for him.

Still, I was convinced that he couldn't be my dad. What kind of person wasn't looking forward to his own wife's return? A phony, part of me said, but the other part knew that if the rumors were true, maybe my dad would be happy to have his freedom.

It couldn't be put off any longer. I needed to call Mom.

CHAPTER SIXTEEN

I had resolved to get up early to call Mom but didn't wake until almost noon. It was nice to be able to sleep in. Grandma had gone to some volunteer committee luncheon and the house was quiet. I calculated the time difference. It was almost nine P.M. in Italy, but I knew Mom would still be up. She worked long hours at home, so I was sure she'd be doing the same in Italy.

She answered her cell on the first ring. "Daisy, can I call you back? I'm in the middle of something." She was talking so softly that I could barely hear her.

"I wouldn't bother you while you're working, but it's important."

"Okay," she replied, "but you'll have to talk fast." There was a strange clanking noise in the background.

"Dad's back in town," I said baldly.

"What?" she sounded breathless.

"He just showed up in Nightshade and moved in with us," I said. "Grandma's staying with us, too."

"Are you sure he's your father?" she asked. I was taken aback by the surprise in her voice. I thought Mom would be the first person to assume he was the real deal.

"I read his mind and he has Dad's memories, but—"

She interrupted me. "He can't be your dad, Daisy," she said. "It's just not possible. Get him out of the house. *Now*."

I got goose bumps from her tone of voice. I figured my mom's psychic abilities had kicked in over the phone and she could sense the truth about the situation. Her insistence, coupled with Mr. Devereaux's, had me convinced.

"I'll make sure he leaves," I said. "And I'll change the locks."

"Good," said Mom. "Now, I'll be out of touch for the next few days. There's no cell phone service where I'm going."

"Where are you going?" I asked.

"I can't talk about that," she said in a low voice. "But Daisy, you and your sisters need to be on your guard. I'll be home as soon as I can." The phone clicked and I realized she'd hung up on me.

I stared at the phone. Something was going on with Mom.

Next, I dialed Poppy and Rose at work and filled them in on what Mom had said. Even Poppy couldn't argue with the fact that Mom was usually right. Rose advised me to call Chief Mendez to come to the house for DoppelDad.

As far as I knew, he was still asleep upstairs, after another one of his late nights. But just as I was about to dial the police station, I heard a noise behind me. I turned, and there he was. DoppelDad had heard everything.

I gasped. I hoped I hadn't made him mad, talking about him behind his back. Who knew what an angry doppelganger was capable of? But DoppelDad just looked more hurt than anything. He turned and ran off, slamming the front door behind him.

Problem solved?

I called Chief Mendez and spilled the whole story, anyway, but DoppelDad was nowhere to be found by the time he got to the house. I kicked myself for not calling him earlier. Now that stranger who looked like my dad was on the loose in Nightshade doing who knows what.

I paced around the house all day, waiting for my sisters to get home from work so I wouldn't feel so vulnerable. Poppy got home first. When our big sister finally made it home from the lab, it was late.

"What took you so long?" Poppy said. She was sprawled out on the couch, cell phone still in hand. She'd spent the evening texting her friend Candy, but when Rose finally showed up, she clicked off the phone. "Daisy and I have been waiting forever."

I took a closer look at Rose's face. It was drawn and pale.

"Poppy, shut up for a second, will you? Can't you see something's wrong?"

Rose drew a shaky breath.

"Rose, sit down. What happened?"

She took a seat on the couch next to Poppy. "Dr. Franken fired me today."

Poppy's jaw dropped.

I had a similar reaction, but also knew Rose was badly shaken up. "I'll make you some tea and then you can tell us all about it."

After making Rose's favorite tea, I added some biscotti to the tray and hurried back into the living room.

Rose had had a shock. A little sugar would be good for her. She'd never been fired from anything before. She was a perfect student and employee.

I handed Rose her cup, then set the tray down on the ottoman between us.

Poppy snagged a biscotti and munched down happily. I smacked her hand. "Those are for Rose."

"There are plenty," she responded, and then stuck out her tongue at me. It was good to see a little of the old Poppy, even if it meant putting up with a little attitude.

"Do you know why she fired you?" I asked.

"That's the horrible part," Rose said. "I don't, not really. Dr. Franken was sweet as pie at first. And she's so brilliant that I didn't even mind all those frivolous errands she sent me on sometimes."

"What changed?"

"I don't know," Rose replied. "She asked about Dad a few

134

weeks ago, and I didn't think anything of it. But then he stopped by the lab today. He looked upset."

"That must have been after he heard me on the phone." I groaned.

"They went into the back room of the lab together for a few minutes," Rose continued.

"Did you follow them?" Poppy asked.

Rose shook her head. "No, I'm not allowed in that part of the lab. But I heard them talking. He mentioned my name."

I wondered why that part of the lab was off-limits, but I let my sister continue her story.

"When Dr. Franken came out, I told her that the person she was talking to wasn't Rafe Giordano, that he was an impostor," Rose said. "I was just trying to help, but Dr. Franken went berserk. She called me a liar. She said she didn't want me working in her lab anymore."

"Dr. Franken is a friend of Dad's," Poppy said. "It makes sense that she would defend him."

"Not really," I said. I went on to tell my sisters what Mr. Devereaux had told me about Dad's relationship with Dr. Franken.

"Well, she sure seemed offended by my calling him a fake," Rose said. "I felt like they were conspiring against me. On my way out of the lab, DoppelDad peeked out from the back and smirked at me. Like he wanted me to be fired."

"Doppelgangers do create chaos," I reminded Rose.

"They sure do," she said, looking crestfallen.

CHAPTER SEVENTEEN

The next day, Rose was still bummed out about losing her job, so Poppy convinced her that a little retail therapy would make her feel better. We were driving to the mall when we saw the smoke coming from the direction of Mrs. Mason's.

"Call 9-1-1," Rose said calmly.

Poppy had her cell phone at the ready, as usual, and punched in the number.

Rose pulled the car over and parked far away from the flames, which seemed to be coming from the greenhouse in the back. As we got out of the car, a soot-covered figure dashed from the rear of the house.

He approached us, out of breath. "Call the fire department," he wheezed. I'd know that voice anywhere. It was Slim.

"Already done."

He was covered in soot, so I could almost make out what he'd look like if he weren't invisible. He was tall and thin, with sharp cheekbones and a narrow jaw. I was thankful to see that he was clothed in baggy trousers and a shirt. He smelled like burnt sugar.

"What happened?" I cried. "Where's Natalie and her grandmother?"

"Natalie's not home," he said, panting.

"Mrs. Mason!" Poppy cried. "We've got to try to save her."

"It's too late," Slim said. He took a long gulp of air. "She was already dead when I found her."

I gasped. "Was it arson?"

He shook his head. "Accident. There was an explosion."

I wanted to ask for more details, but the Nightshade Volunteer Fire Department arrived and set to work. One of the firefighters said it was too late for the greenhouse, but they'd try to save the main house.

The fire crept closer, so we retreated to a safer distance, where we were standing when Chief Mendez arrived. To my surprise, Mr. Bone was with him.

"What happened?" Mr. Bone said to Slim.

Slim didn't say anything, but his glance at us spoke volumes.

"Does this have anything to do with the doppelgangers?" I asked Slim. "Flo told me you were doing undercover work."

"Way to blow my cover, sis," he said sarcastically.

Mr. Bone chuckled. "The Giordanos already know most of the council's business. And what they don't already know, they do a pretty good job guessing."

Slim nodded. He cleared his throat. "The council's suspicions were correct. Mrs. Mason was making the doppelgangers, using witchcraft."

Poppy looked incredulous. "One little old lady caused all this madness?"

Chief Mendez looked thoughtful. "We think Mrs. Mason had help. Did you ever see her with anyone unusual?"

I recalled the time we saw Natalie's grandma arguing with Dr. Franken. But then again, Mrs. Mason argued with everybody.

"We saw Mrs. Mason at the college," Poppy said.

"She volunteers at the campus arboretum," Rose replied.

"Any idea why she was at the lab when we stopped by?" I asked.

Rose gave me a sharp glance. "No idea."

"Or why she was arguing with Dr. Franken?"

"Dr. Franken didn't have anything to do with Mrs. Mason's death," Rose insisted. "Slim said it was an accident."

"I said it was an explosion," he said. "From what I could see in the short time I was in the greenhouse, it was an accident."

"How did you find her?" I asked.

"My . . . unusual circumstances allow me to move about undetected," Slim replied. "I was observing Mrs. Mason in the greenhouse when the explosion occurred."

"How did it happen?" Poppy asked.

Mr. Bone said, "It most assuredly happened while Mrs.

Mason was practicing magic. The spell to create doppelgangers takes a lot of energy and is quite volatile."

Slim explained, "The spell got away from her. The whole room took on a green glow. It let out a tremendous amount of heat and then I heard a popping noise as the glass in the greenhouse shattered."

"Then what happened?" Poppy prompted.

"Everything went black. When I woke up, I was on the ground and there was fire all around me. I saw a little bit of pink. It was Mrs. Mason's jogging suit. I tried to get her out of there, but she was pinned under a potting table. Just her sneakers were peeking out."

"Why would she create doppelgangers to create havoc in Nightshade?" I asked. "Especially since she was part of the council."

"That's a good question," Chief Mendez said. "She'd become bitter in the last few years, since her son, Natalie's father, was killed. She blamed the council for his death, but I never thought she would actually turn against us."

"Do you think this will be the end of it?" I asked. "What will happen to all the doppelgangers?"

"I don't know," Slim said. "But I don't think Mrs. Mason was working alone."

"You don't think it was *Natalie?*" I was horrified by the thought.

"There's no way," he said. "I'm absolutely sure that it's not

Natalie. Her grandmother wouldn't let her near the greenhouse. Besides, Natalie's a good person."

"Speaking of Natalie," Chief Mendez said, "I'd better find her. Someone needs to tell her about her grandmother's death."

"I'll go with you," Slim said. "She can stay with me for a few days."

He and Chief Mendez left. I stood staring after them, thinking about what had just happened.

I agreed with Slim. It couldn't be Natalie, but, then, who was it? "Maybe now we'll find out who else is out to get the Nightshade City Council," I said. But I wasn't sure we really would. I had a dreadful feeling that, this time, the bad guy had outsmarted all of us.

CHAPTER EIGHTEEN

Mrs. Mason's funeral was held early in the morning a few days later. Slim asked my sisters and me to attend. Grandma came with us, but there was no sign of our father figure. Word of Mrs. Mason's involvement in the doppelganger scare had spread and the paranormal community avoided her burial.

The service was held at Mort's, of course, but besides my family, and Nicholas and his dad, who kind of had to be there, only Ryan and his dad showed.

"Daisy, thanks so much for coming," Natalie said. She gave me a hug. It looked like she'd been crying for days.

Natalie was surprisingly composed during the service, but when it was time to leave, she broke down and Slim led her away.

"What will she do now?" I asked Chief Mendez.

"Slim will take care of her," he said. "Natalie didn't do anything wrong."

"But that hasn't stopped the paranormal community from

avoiding her," I said. "Bad or good, Natalie loved her grandmother." It wasn't fair.

Ryan put his arm around me. "We won't avoid her."

I smiled and leaned in to him. "You're the best."

Ryan came over afterward and we made a cake to take over to Slim's later. It was the only thing I could think of to show Natalie that we wouldn't abandon her.

It took a tragedy to make it happen, but things were back to normal with me and Ryan. He forgave me for lying about DoppelDad. After all, all bets were off when it came to family. Ryan even admitted to me that he would have probably done the same thing if his mom—or a doppelganger of her—showed up at his house.

I was surprised when DoppelDad showed up at our house again late that afternoon, after Ryan had left for football practice. DoppelDad had to knock this time, since we had the locks changed. I didn't know where he'd been, but there were rumors of him being spotted with various gorgeous young women (although, thankfully, not Natalie) all over town.

"Hi," I said cautiously.

"I heard you're going through some tough times," he said. "I thought we might spend some time together."

I toyed with the idea of slamming the door in his face after what he'd done to Rose, or of calling Chief Mendez, but the desperation in his voice tugged at my heartstrings. He was dressed as my father might have been on a Saturday afternoon: khaki shorts, a faded T-shirt, and a UC Nightshade hooded sweatshirt. Sometimes it was still hard to believe that I wasn't really looking at my own father.

"Want to walk to the beach?" I asked, figuring it would be safer to talk to him in public.

"Sure," he said.

It was a long walk, but the idea was to get him to talk. And besides, Poppy was working at the Snack Shack, so she'd be there for reinforcement, if needed.

We walked in silence, but finally my curiosity got the better of me. "Where have you been lately?"

"With a friend," he replied.

Not exactly forthcoming.

We finally reached the beach. It was the middle of summer and we'd have an audience. Half of Nightshade, the non-nocturnal half, was at the beach.

It didn't seem to bother DoppelDad, though. He smiled pleasantly at everyone who greeted him by my father's name.

The whispers and stares didn't seem to bother him, but they were definitely getting to me.

"I'll get us something from the snack bar," I offered. "What would you like?"

He clapped his hands like a little kid. "Do they have cotton candy?"

"I'm sure they do. Wait here. I'll be right back."

He settled on a bench with a clear view of the water while I went to get the snacks.

The Snack Shack was busy and Poppy couldn't really talk. So I made it quick.

"DoppelDad's here," I said.

"Has he said anything about where he's been?"

"Not really. He wants cotton candy."

"Hmm. That's what Mrs. Wilder's doppelganger gobbled down," Poppy said.

"I know, spooky, huh?"

"I dunno," she said. "Everyone likes cotton candy in the summer. We've been selling tons of it. It can't all be to doppelgangers." She handed me the sticky treat. "Anything else?"

"A chocolate-dipped cone?"

I handed her my money, and she said, "Daisy?"

"Yes?"

"Can you guys hang until I can take a break? Just so I can say hi?"

The note of yearning made me ashamed of myself about suspecting him. For Poppy's sake, I hoped he *was* our dad. So our dad wasn't perfect. I tried not to let it bother me that our real dad might be a player. That didn't mean he didn't love us. Did it?

Besides, people changed and he'd been held captive all those years. No wonder he wanted to kick up his heels a little. That didn't mean he was cheating on Mom.

"Of course! We'll hang out until your break."

As I walked back, I heard Samantha calling my name. She waved at me from a bright pink beach towel, so I cut through the sand to go say hi.

I was halfway there when I noticed that she was accompanied by Sean and several of his new and obnoxious buddies from the football team.

"Daisy, want to join us?"

"Uh, no, thanks. I'm with someone." I took a lick of my chocolate cone.

Wolfgang snorted gleefully and I turned and glared at him.

My ire didn't seem to faze Wolfie at all. "Trolling for dates?" he asked.

I glared at him.

Sean nudged him and said, "Let's go throw the ball. See ya, Daisy."

He wouldn't meet my eyes and I could understand why. I wouldn't want to be seen with Wolfgang Paxton, either, especially not after the way he acted at the movies.

I wondered if Ryan knew that Sean was still hanging out with Wolfie.

After they left, I turned to Samantha. "I can't stand not knowing for sure if that guy is my father."

I pointed to where he stood ogling Mrs. Justus, who was smokin' hot and *almost* age appropriate.

"Just hang in there until you guys figure out what's going on," she said. "Have you talked to the council?"

"Not officially," I said. "But Rose has been updating Nicholas and his father."

"Why haven't the council acted?" she asked.

"There's not much else they can do. They know that Mrs. Mason was the one who created the doubles, but they think she had help. There's someone following the doppelgangers around in the hopes that it'll eventually lead to whoever was helping her."

We were silent for a minute. We watched as Wolfgang purposefully tripped one of his cronies and rubbed sand in his face.

"Why is Sean hanging out with that guy? He's a creep."

"He's okay," she said. "A little aggressive, maybe."

"A little?" I said incredulously. "He's a menace."

As if to prove my point, Wolfgang threw the football right at a couple of little harpy kids. If you looked really closely, you could see the nubs of their baby wings. The youngest started to cry, and her older brother, who was barely old enough to toddle, extended his claws and glared at Wolfie, who just laughed.

"Why is he such a jerk?" I asked.

Samantha avoided my eyes. "I don't know," she said. "Sean's my boyfriend, but it's not like I can tell him who to be friends with."

"I know," I said, "but Wolfgang is so obnoxious. Just look at him. Next he'll be kicking sand in the faces of little old ladies."

Sam sighed. "I don't know what to do," she admitted. "Sean won't listen to me. He's been really moody lately and hardly has any time for me."

I was surprised by this. Samantha was gorgeous, one of the most popular girls in school, and she had Sean wrapped around her little finger.

"Give him some time," I advised. "But try to get him to spend less time with Wolfie. Maybe you and Sean and Ryan and I can go out again soon? We haven't done that in ages."

"I'd like that," she said.

"I've got to get back," I said, nodding toward where *he* still sat on the bench.

I wandered back over and handed DoppelDad an enormous mound of cotton candy. I expected him to gulp it down, but instead, he tore off a strip and offered it to me.

"No thanks."

He shrugged and popped it into his mouth. "Were those your friends?"

I shrugged. "Some of them. Would you like something else?" I asked. "Poppy works at the Snack Shack, over there." I pointed to the stand.

Poppy saw us and took off her apron before heading our way. "I'm taking a break," she called to her coworkers before she left the shack.

I wandered a little, to give her some time alone with Doppel-Dad. When I came back, they were sitting at a picnic table and DoppelDad had a cup of soft serve ice cream in front of him.

Poppy bounded over to meet me. "It is him, I'm sure of it," she crowed. "It's Dad."

"But Poppy, we talked about this—"

"But he was being so nice just now," she said. "Just like Dad used to be. He even said he'd talk to Dr. Franken about getting Rose her job back."

"If he was our real dad, he never would have gotten her fired in the first place," I snapped.

Poppy was grasping at straws. "Well, how else would he have known about my hair?" she challenged.

"Remember, doppelgangers retain memories of the original. Besides, there are always family photos, school yearbook, a million possibilities."

"Stop it, Daisy. I'm beginning to think you don't want him to be Dad. That you don't want him to come home. Well, I do."

So did I, more than anything. But I couldn't bear the disappointment if he turned out to be a phony.

I sighed. "We've got to prove this once and for all," I said. "I'm going to invite him over for dinner."

Poppy brightened. "That's a great idea, Daisy!"

I lowered my voice. "And then when he shows up, we're going to have Chief Mendez come over and take him away for testing."

Poppy's face fell. "You can't, Daisy!" she said. "You can't let them put our father in a cage like they did to Miss McBennett at the council meeting."

"That wasn't Miss McBennett. That was her doppelganger," I gently reminded her. "And if this guy is a doppelganger, this will just prove it. If not, no harm done."

"You promise that they won't hurt him?" Poppy said.

"Chief Mendez gave me his word," I said.

Finally, Poppy agreed that it was the only solution. She returned to work and I strode back to DoppelDad.

"Hey, Dad, would you like to come over for dinner?" I asked, with my best fake smile on.

He looked a little taken aback. "Uh, sure," he said. "When?"

"How's tomorrow night?"

"No good. I have other plans."

My anger started boiling up but I kept it under control. "Okay, the next night, then," I said sweetly. "We can even make the meal together, just like we used to do."

DoppelDad accepted the invitation, then made a hasty exit when he spotted an ice cream truck approaching.

CHAPTER NINETEEN

On Saturday night, Ryan was at my house, helping me make cookies. Well, he was helping me eat them, anyway.

"Do you mind if we hang out with Samantha and Sean tonight?" I asked. "I invited them over. I haven't seen much of either of them lately." I was hoping a little quality time together would help Sean and Ryan drop whatever beef they had.

"Sure, that would be great," Ryan said. But I could tell by his expression that something was bothering him. I gave him an inquiring look.

"Things haven't been so great between Sean and me lately, ever since he started hanging out with Wolfgang. He barely even talks to me at practice anymore."

"He's your best friend," I said.

"He *was* my best friend," Ryan replied. "But I'm not sure he still is."

"Of course he is!" I said, truly alarmed now.

"I hope tonight will help," Ryan said. "He acts like he's mad at me."

"About what?"

"That's just it. He won't tell me. Whenever I ask him about it, he just says nothing is wrong."

"Samantha says he hasn't been acting like himself to her, either. Do you know what's going on with him? He's as moody as you were when you were going through your . . . change."

"But Sean's not a Were," Ryan pointed out reasonably.

"Not that we know of," I muttered.

"What do you mean?"

"It's just that Nicholas mentioned that werewolves could be made," I said.

Ryan looked horrified. "Yes, but no one in their right mind would do something like that."

"Wolfie might," I said. "Maybe Sean's just going along with it."

"Why?" Ryan sounded skeptical. "That doesn't sound like Sean at all. He's a good guy."

I shrugged. I didn't know, but I intended to find out.

About an hour later, Sam and Sean were on my doorstep. I invited them in and gave Sam a big hug. "I feel like I haven't seen you all summer," I said.

"I know," she said. "But we've both been busy with our new jobs and the guys have been busy with football."

151

"How is football going?" I asked Sean casually.

"Okay," Sean muttered. I noticed that he didn't make eye contact with Ryan. Something was definitely wrong. I looked at Sam, but she just shrugged.

I changed the subject. "Are you guys hungry? I made cookies."

Sean looked at his hand. "I already ate."

Samantha elbowed him sharply. "I mean, thank you, but I've already eaten," Sean said.

"How about a game of Scrabble?" Ryan suggested.

I winced. Sean was notoriously bad at spelling, but to my surprise, he brightened. "That's a good idea."

We sat on the rug in the living room and set up the game. But the evening deteriorated quickly when the first word Sean spelled out was *liar*. He glared at Ryan as the points were tallied, but Ryan was doing his best to ignore it.

Sean's next word was either *furry* or *fury*, but I didn't have a chance to verify it before Ryan knocked the tiles off the board.

"What's your problem?" he said to Sean. The tendons in his neck stood out. "You've been acting like an ass all summer."

"You're the one with the problem," Sean replied. "You wanna take this outside?"

Ryan nodded. "If that's what you want. Are you going to get your little pal Wolfie to help you?" he said mockingly.

"At least Wolfie is honest," Sean shot back.

"Guys," Sam said. "Knock it off. You're friends."

"That's what I thought," Sean said. "I thought we were best

friends, but evidently, we're not. Best friends tell each other everything."

"What haven't I told you?" Ryan demanded.

Sean stared at him and got to his feet. "Did it slip your mind that you turn furry and howl at the moon once a month? A little information you might have shared with your *best friend*." With that, he turned and left the house.

There was silence in the room for a minute, then Ryan said, "I can't believe I didn't tell him."

"Well, someone did," Samantha said. "Wolfgang."

Frankly, I couldn't believe it, either, but now was not the time to tell my boyfriend that. "Go after him," I urged. "Just explain it."

"Good idea," Ryan said. "At least I can try."

After they both were gone, Samantha and I looked at each other for a minute.

"Boys," she said, after the long silence. "They're so moody." And then shrugged, and grabbed a cookie.

We spent an hour playing Scrabble, but neither of the guys came back. Finally, Samantha and I called it a night.

"Do you think they made up?" she said before she left.

"They had to have," I said. "They're best friends, aren't they?"

"I don't know," she said. "They were both really angry, and Sean does some stupid things when he's mad."

It wasn't long before we found out exactly how stupid Sean could be.

CHAPTER TWENTY

For the big night of our "family" dinner with Dad, my sisters and I had decided on barbecued chicken, homemade potato salad, and watermelon, with chocolate cake for dessert. Grandma insisted on giving us money for groceries, so Poppy and I headed to the grocery store to buy the ingredients.

We were in the meat section when she nudged me. "Isn't that Wolfgang Paxton?" she said in a whisper. "What is he doing? Harassing the butcher?"

I laughed, but sobered quickly. I wouldn't put it past him.

He was standing at the meat counter, where the butcher handed him several large items wrapped in white paper. His cart was piled high.

"Evidently, buying enough raw meat to feed an army," I replied.

There was quite a line, so Poppy and I patiently waited our turn. Wolfgang was still loading up his cart when I noticed Sean approaching him.

Poppy noticed, too. "I've never seen Sean look so angry," she said.

He and Wolfie had engaged in a low-voiced conversation, and it was clear from the expressions on their faces and their body language that they were arguing. I strained to hear, but it was too noisy in the store and they were speaking much too quietly.

Wolfgang openly smirked at Sean and then gave him a little shove. It took some nerve to get physical with Sean, who was a big guy. Of course, Wolfgang was a werewolf, which gave him an advantage, but my money was still on Sean.

The guy was completely out of control.

I was startled when Sean jabbed his finger into Wolfie's chest for emphasis and then strode away. Wolfgang didn't even flinch, but I saw him gazing after Sean with a look of hatred. He looked up and caught me staring. His lip curled back into a nasty smile and I looked away. When I looked up again, he was gone.

I gave the butcher our order, then Poppy and I went to the next aisle to finish the shopping, but my mind was busy. I looked down and realized that I'd managed to float a couple of bars of chocolate into the cart without even realizing.

I looked up at Poppy. "Hey, did you pick those up?"

She giggled. "No, you did. And I think you almost gave Mr. Hanson a heart attack when he saw those chocolates float by."

"Oops, I'd better pay better attention," I said. I didn't want everyone in Nightshade to know I had telekinetic powers.

What were Wolfgang and Sean talking about? It had looked like they were arguing. Was Sean somehow involved in the rogue pack?

I had put the questions out of my mind by the time Poppy and I got home. We were already behind schedule, so I put the chicken in marinade and started the chocolate cake.

Rose and Poppy decided to hang out in the backyard with me while I cooked the chicken. I didn't have much experience using our barbecue, but I'd learned a lot from Slim, so I had confidence that I wouldn't burn the chicken.

I managed to get dinner ready in time. Despite the fact that our DoppelDad was a no-show, I was pleased to see that Grandma was enjoying herself. She had been glum ever since he had left the house. I didn't want to think about how she was going to react when she found out that he wasn't her son.

Grandma said, "Daisy, that was delicious. Thank you."

Everyone commented on how good the potato salad was and I glowed with pride.

"Slim gave me the recipe," I admitted. "But he said I can't reveal the secret ingredient."

Rose laughed. "As long as it's not magical, I don't care. Just keep making it!"

It was a close, humid night, and although it was getting dark by the time we'd finished our meal, no one felt like going inside yet. Poppy and Rose and I took the dirty plates into the kitchen and then I sliced up the chocolate cake and brought it back outside on a tray.

"I forgot the pitcher of milk," I said.

"Sit down," Rose commanded. "I'll get it."

I took a seat in my favorite Adirondack chair and leaned back contentedly. It felt like we were in for a summer storm, but there was a slight breeze blowing.

Rose appeared with the pitcher of cold milk. A second later, I heard a growl and a large animal bounded out of the shrubbery and went flying toward her. She screamed but kept a death grip on the pitcher.

It was a shaggy gray wolf. His fangs were bared and he moved so quickly, I could barely breathe, let alone think. Poppy saved the day. With a quick look, she sent the glass pitcher flying. It hit the wolf squarely on the head and knocked it out. Milk ran down its motionless face.

We were frozen in shock for a few minutes.

"Why the sudden interest from the werewolf community?" I wondered aloud when I finally found my voice again.

Poppy asked, "Is it dead?"

"I don't think so," Rose said. "Just unconscious."

"Go get some rope from the garage. And hurry," Grandma said to Poppy.

"Rose, sit down," I said. "You look like you're going to faint." She did as I told her. Her face was as white as the milk.

Poppy came back with the rope. The animal hadn't stirred, but I was still surprised when Grandma grabbed the rope.

"Be careful!" I said.

"Don't worry," she said. "When I'm done, this wolf won't be able to move. Poppy, call Nicholas and tell him to come over. We have a problem."

A big hairy problem.

While Poppy dialed Nicholas, I stared up at the sky. There was no sign of a full moon, which convinced me that this was a young wolf, maybe even one of the pack we'd seen before. But why did they keep coming back to our house?

"Obviously, someone has it out for the Giordano family." I hadn't realized that I said it aloud, until Poppy gave me a dirty look.

I clapped a hand over my mouth. We had tried to protect Grandma from as much of Nightshade's weirdness as possible, but by the calm, efficient way she was trussing up the werewolf, our protective behavior might not have been necessary. She evidently wasn't fazed by much, including a visit from someone from the supernatural community.

Nicholas must have broken a few traffic laws, because we barely had the wolf tied up before he arrived.

"Rose, are you okay?" he said. She stood up shakily and he took her into his arms.

"I'm fine. Poppy saved me with a pitcher of milk. Good thing Daisy doesn't like plastic," she joked weakly.

Nicholas looked over at the werewolf. Grandma had him tied up as neatly as she wrapped our Christmas presents.

"What should we do with him?" Rose said.

"I'll take him to the garage," Nicholas said. "I have a feeling that the wolf will be shifting back to its human form soon and then we'll know who is behind this bad behavior."

Nicholas grabbed the werewolf and lifted it easily. His super strength came in handy.

It occurred to me that that kind of strength could come in handy for football, and I wondered again if this Were was someone on the team.

The rest of us trooped to the garage after Nicholas, although I noticed Poppy managed to scoop up a slice of chocolate cake before she exited.

Nicholas found a couple of old towels and draped them over the creature for modesty's sake. I wasn't sure whose modesty he was trying to protect, ours or the wolf's, but either way, when the creature regained its human form, now it wouldn't do so naked.

About an hour later, the transformation began. I thought I'd see Wolfgang Paxton. But I was as surprised as everyone else when I saw who it was.

"Sean?" I said.

Wait until Ryan heard about this.

CHAPTER TWENTY-ONE

"Sean?" I said again. I was having trouble processing the information.

We untied him and he sat up and put a hand to his head, wincing. I caught him looking down, and noted the relief on his face when he realized he was covered by a blanket.

"Where am I?" he said.

"At our house," Poppy said.

He looked blank.

Poppy continued, "But the real question is, why are you here?"

Nicholas grabbed his cell phone and started to dial. "I have to call my father. The council needs to know there's a new werewolf in town."

"The council?" Sean paled. "What will they do to me? I wasn't trying to hurt anyone . . . I just smelled the meat on the barbecue and lost control."

"Then why did you try to attack Rose?" Nicholas replied. "The council frowns on that kind of behavior."

Rose put her hand on Nicholas's arm. "Let's hear what he has to say first."

Nicholas said, "Okay, start talking."

Sean still looked shaken, but he'd lost some of his bravado. He pulled himself together. "I think it was the experiments."

"What kind of experiments?" Poppy asked.

He kept mute.

"Sean, it's important that you tell us the truth. We might be able to help you."

He wouldn't meet my eyes, but at least he started talking. "Experimenting with 'roids."

"Steroids?" Rose shot me a horrified look.

Sean nodded gravely.

"Are you a complete idiot?" Poppy blurted. "That stuff is dangerous."

He coughed and a little ball of hair, probably from the pelt of a rabbit, came out of his mouth and landed on the floor. He stared at it, appalled at his social gaffe.

"I'll get you a glass of water, and some ice for your head," Grandma said as she left the garage.

She hurried back a few minutes later with an ice pack and a drink for our guest. As she handed it to him, she asked quickly, "Did I miss anything?"

I shook my head. Sean had been mute, staring at the rabbit fur on the floor the whole time she was gone.

Now he emptied the glass in one gulp, then sighed. "Thank

161

you. At first I just used regular steroids. But it wasn't working. I wasn't big enough to . . ."

"Compete with the Weres on the football team," I guessed. "Go on," I prompted him.

"But pretty soon, it wasn't just traditional steroids," he continued. "It was something much worse."

"Worse? How much worse?" Poppy said.

"I started using what he called a hairball. A hairball is a mixture of traditional steroids and . . ."

"And what?" Nicholas prompted him again.

"Were blood," Sean replied. He hung his head.

Rose gasped. "That's terrible. Why did you do it?"

"I just wanted to see what it was like. If my best friend could be a werewolf, why couldn't I? But pretty soon I was shifting almost every night, not just when the moon was full."

"Where'd you get the hairballs?" I asked.

Sean shook his head. "I can't say."

But I'd already guessed. "Wolfie has been a very naughty boy," I said.

Nicholas picked up his phone. "Definitely council business," he said. "I'll call Dad. He needs to know about this."

"Excuse us for a moment," Poppy said to Sean. He simply nodded and repositioned the ice pack that was against his head. The rest of us followed her to a spot in the garage, out of his earshot.

"What are they going to do with Wolfgang?" I asked Rose.

"I don't care. You heard what he said. That creep is injecting people to turn them into werewolves. Sean's just a victim." Sean was our next-door neighbor, so she had watched him grow up. I knew she had a soft spot for him. But the truth is, he wasn't just a victim. He'd made the decision to go along with Wolfgang, and the damage might be permanent.

Poppy groaned. "I just can't believe Sean would do steroids. Or hairballs. Whatever."

Nicholas finished his conversation with his father and hung up. "Dad and Chief Mendez are going to the Paxtons' in a few minutes. I'll take Sean there to meet them."

"I've got to tell Samantha," I said.

"What can we do to help?" Rose asked.

"Hope that the council is able to find a cure for this. I don't think Sean knew what he was getting into. But I do know there's a whole pack of teen werewolves running around, and after what we learned tonight, I'm pretty sure they are on the football team."

"Let's go inside before any more surprise visitors show up," Grandma said. "And I'll get that poor boy some of your father's clothes."

She left the garage as I pondered the fact that Mom still had some of Dad's stuff. We'd helped her bag up a bunch of it to donate it. I had thought that that meant she was resolved he wasn't coming back. But maybe she had just done it to appease us. I wondered where his clothes had ended up. A glimmer of a memory teased the edge of my mind, but I couldn't grasp it. I'd seen piles of clothing lately, and it wasn't just in Poppy's room. The memory eluded me.

Nicholas extended a hand and helped Sean to his feet, none too gently. He grabbed the blanket as it started to slip, then blushed profusely.

Poppy and I made a quick exit from the garage before we embarrassed the guy any further.

We congregated in the living room to wait for Grandma to come back with something for Sean to wear. He made sure he had a firm grip on the blanket when he joined us.

She returned just as the silence was moving from uncomfortable to completely awkward. Handing Sean a stack of men's clothing, she said, "Nicholas, please show our guest where he can change," which meant Nicholas should guard the bathroom door while Sean got dressed. Although Sean's story made a horrible kind of sense, it was not completely clear that the attack was unintentional.

Wolfgang Paxton was a bad combination of arrogance and inexperience. I could picture him creating new werewolves just for the malicious pleasure of it. But I couldn't figure out why a decent guy like Sean would go along with it.

Were they that desperate to win a championship?

I wanted privacy to give Ryan the heads-up on Sean's involvement.

When I called him and told him the story, as briefly as possible, Ryan sounded grim. "The football team? Are you sure?"

"Not certain about all, but at least some of them. Probably freshman string," I said, guessing that those boys would be the most easily influenced by Wolfgang.

"And . . ." I hesitated. It was going to be hard for Ryan to hear that Sean was involved, but Ryan knew he had been hanging around Wolfie a lot.

"And Sean," Ryan finished for me. "I'll be right over."

When I answered the door a little later, I was expecting only Ryan, but next to him stood a very irritated Samantha Devereaux.

"Er, hi, everyone. Come on in."

I held the door open and they followed me to the living room.

Sean sat on the loveseat. There was room next to him, but Sam very pointedly chose a seat far away from her boyfriend.

Ryan sat next to me on the ottoman. "Did I miss anything?"

Sean sat in silence, but Samantha glared at him.

He was in for it now. Samantha was fuming, I could tell.

Sean cleared his throat. Sam gave him a look and he started talking. "I've been hanging around Wolfgang."

"Everyone knows that," Sam said impatiently. "Get to the point."

Pretty soon, the whole sorry story came out.

"He said the hairballs would improve my game," Sean said. "I told myself I would only try it once, but then I saw a difference—I got stronger and faster, quick. I knew it was wrong.

Good thing I stopped. Some of the guys are having . . . problems. Worse than me, if you can believe it."

"Sean!" Sam snapped. "I can't believe you were dumb enough to fall for that."

He hung his head in shame and mumbled some apologies.

"I'm going to kill him," Samantha said.

"Killing a werewolf isn't easy," I joked weakly. "You'd better stock up on silver bullets."

She flinched.

"I'm sorry," I said. "That was insensitive."

"Thanks, Daisy," Sam said. "But even if Sean only did it *once*, that's bad enough."

"I didn't let Wolfgang inject me anymore," Sean said, "at least not after I saw what it did to me."

"What did it do?" Poppy said.

"At first, it seemed like some kind of miracle," Sean admitted. "These skinny little freshmen bulked up almost overnight. Pretty soon they were lifting the same amount as me." He sounded aggrieved. "I was tempted to keep on using it, believe me. But then we started seeing the side effects."

"What side effects?" Poppy said.

"At first, it was just hair. Lots of hair," Sean said. "But then they started to change, and not just once in a while." He turned to Nicholas and asked with a pleading note in his voice, "Is it reversible?"

Nicholas said, "Possibly." He looked at Ryan. "There's a doctor in town who specializes in Were issues." He was talking about the doctor Rose had taken him to last spring when Ryan had abruptly changed and challenged Nicholas. In the heat of the moment, Nicholas had been injured.

Sean shuddered. "I hope they can reverse it. After we started changing, some of the guys wanted to stop. But Wolfgang convinced us that this was the only way we were going to take the championship." He looked at Ryan when he said it.

Ryan shuddered. "I don't want to win like this," he said. "But why did he pick you? Why didn't you tell me?"

Ryan took my hand as we all listened to the rest of Sean's story.

"I was . . . upset that you hadn't told me you were a werewolf," Sean admitted to Ryan. "Wolfie told me what was going on with you. I thought I might learn something about werewolves by hanging around with him and his crew. I thought it might help me understand what you were going through. But I got in way over my head."

"I'm sorry, Sean," Ryan said. "I meant to tell you, but—"

"It's all good," Sean said quickly. "Friends again?" He extended his hand and Ryan shook it vigorously.

"Friends."

The impromptu meeting finally broke up.

Nicholas got to his feet. "I've got to go. I have to make a stop at the Paxton residence. There's a certain wolf cub who needs schooling. And we have to see what we can do for this idiot." He grabbed Sean by the collar and steered him toward the door.

Samantha followed them out. Through our open windows, I could hear her scolding Sean as they walked to Nicholas's car. He wasn't getting off easy on this one.

I kissed Ryan goodbye. After the house emptied out, I headed for bed, but I couldn't sleep. I wondered if the guys on the team would be okay or if the injections would have permanent side effects. I hoped that Wolfgang Paxton was thoroughly ashamed of himself. If he wasn't now, he would be by the time the Nightshade City Council was through with him.

CHAPTER TWENTY-TWO

Nicholas gave us word later that the Nightshade City Council had things well in hand. The doctor had said that it would require a series of painful treatments, but the guys on the football team might eventually return to normal.

Now that the rogue werewolf pack mystery had been resolved, I was focused on DoppelDad again. I couldn't take the suspense anymore.

I was off from work the next day, so Ryan and I had decided to go looking for him.

When Ryan rang the doorbell that afternoon, I was ready, but barely. I hadn't gotten much sleep the night before and hadn't woken up before noon.

"I forgot to pack a picnic," I confessed to him after our hello kiss. I was supposed to be in charge of snacks.

"That's okay," he said. "We can swing by Slim's later, unless you're sick of it by now."

"I love Slim's potato salad, and we could grab a couple of panini sandwiches. He just added those to the menu."

"Sounds great," Ryan said. "Where should we look first?"

"Let's try places that sell sweets, like the concession stand at the beach or even the Donut Hole. Like the other doppelgangers, DoppelDad seems to have a thing for sweets."

He wasn't at any of the places I'd thought of, although we did stop at Slim's to look for him there—and to grab some food to eat "on stake-out," as Ryan jokingly called it.

"What about Mrs. Mason's?" Ryan suggested. "You said you'd followed him there."

"Well, the greenhouse where she created the doppelgangers went up in smoke, but it's worth a try," I said.

Ryan put the car in gear and we headed to Natalie's grandma's house.

The flower garden in the front was nearly black, the plants dead or dying. Even the roses, Mrs. Mason's pride and joy, were wilted.

The lawn looked like it hadn't been watered in weeks. "Natalie doesn't have her grandma's green thumb," I commented.

"Or the magic died with Mrs. Mason," Ryan replied.

I hadn't thought of that, but it supported the suspicions about Mrs. Mason's beating Mom out for prize ribbons for her plants at the county fair every year.

Ryan parked. "It doesn't look like anybody's home," he said.

I knew Natalie had been staying at Slim's, so I figured there was little chance of her returning to her grandma's house while we were there. "Let's check out back," I suggested.

"Ryan, there he is!" We ducked behind a large potted plant near the patio before DoppelDad could spot us. There was barely room for the both of us, so I ended up pressed against his chest. Not a bad place to be.

DoppelDad was dressed in khaki pants, a blue button-down shirt, and a blazer. Something about the outfit looked familiar. Suddenly I realized where I'd seen it before—he was wearing a replica of an outfit Dad wore in one of our family photos.

He looked around furtively and then crossed the garden to the path leading to the charred remains of the greenhouse.

Ryan and I crept after him. When we reached the blackened door, Ryan held it open for me. I moved as quietly as possible, but tripped over a sprinkler line and nearly fell. Ryan caught me and probably prevented me from breaking my leg or something.

Most of the glass that had made up the walls and ceiling of the greenhouse was broken or gone completely from the force of the explosion. What was left was covered in ash, obscuring the light and making it difficult to see across the long room.

There was no movement in the greenhouse. DoppelDad couldn't have just vanished. Ryan and I crept along the length of the room, checking under the sooty metal potting tables that remained. Then, at the far end of the greenhouse, we came to a large hole in the ground. It looked like it could be an entrance to a tunnel.

There were fresh footprints in the blackened soil leading into the opening. It must have been where DoppelDad had disappeared. "I wonder if this tunnel had something to do with her doppelganger-making operation," I said.

"Hold on a minute," Ryan told me.

He ran out to the car and came back with his cell phone, a large flashlight, and a large white paper bag, which I assumed contained our dinner. He also had a sweatshirt, which he handed me. "Put this on. It's cold underground."

"Thanks," I said. "But what about you?"

"I'll be okay. I'm leaving a message with Dad about what we're doing," he said. "This tunnel could lead anywhere." He opened his cell and left a brief message with his dad.

"Okay, let's go." He shone the light into the tunnel. It was narrow at first, but we could see that it gradually increased in size until it became large enough to stand up in, with smooth, slime-covered walls.

"I wonder if Natalie knew anything about this tunnel," Ryan said.

"I doubt it," I assured him. "She told me that her grandmother never let anyone in her greenhouse. Even her own granddaughter."

"It looks like it's been here a long time. What do you think it is?"

"I don't know. Maybe a sewage pipe or something?"

I flinched at the thought. "Gross."

"We don't have to go in," he said. "We could call Dad and he'll have his deputy check it out."

"No, I want to," I said. "I need to know exactly what my dad's double is up to."

Ryan led the way, but held my hand and helped me over any rough spots. We both had to walk stooped over because the tunnel wasn't big enough for us to stand completely upright.

I wondered if the smell bothered him. It bothered me and I didn't have the extremely sensitive nose of a werewolf.

The flashlight illuminated candy wrappers, a bunch of discarded donut boxes, and a particularly rude bit of graffiti, but nothing else. There was no sign of DoppelDad, but we hadn't found any possible exits, either, so obviously he was still somewhere ahead of us.

The tunnel widened and turned, and then there was finally plenty of room for Ryan and me to stand upright.

"We have to be getting close now," I said. It felt like we'd been walking for hours, but my watch said we'd only been in the tunnel about twenty minutes.

"Close to what?" Ryan replied. A few minutes later, he stopped and held a finger to his lips. Werewolves hear better than humans, too.

"Do you hear it?" His lips barely moved.

"Hear what?" I whispered back.

"Voices."

I didn't hear anything, but I took his word for it. We started walking again, this time more cautiously. After we went a few feet more, I could hear the voices, too, but I couldn't understand anything they were saying.

Ryan shone his flashlight on a small door built into the bricks directly in front of us. There was a thin trickle of light coming from behind it.

We waited for the sounds of the voices to recede, and eventually, there was silence on the other side of the wall.

"Do you think it's safe?" I asked, careful to keep my voice low.

"I haven't heard anything," Ryan said, which was reassuring. He'd pick something up before I would. "Do you sense anything?"

Meaning, I guess, that I should try to use my psychic abilities to see if I could glean anything. I shrugged. I had been practicing, so maybe there was a chance I'd be able to hear someone else's thoughts. I was no Rose, though.

I put my ear to the wall and concentrated, but all I got was the distressing feeling that there was now something slimy in my hair. "Nothing," I finally said. "I'm not picking up any thoughts at all."

"That probably means the room's empty now," Ryan said. "Let's go."

I held my breath, unsure what we'd find.

He handed me the flashlight, which I trained on the door while he fumbled with the latch. The door creaked open.

As we stepped inside, I realized we were in a lab of some kind. It looked eerily similar to a place I'd been before.

The room was in shadow, but I could see the outlines of beakers, test tubes, and other lab equipment. The trash cans were piled high with pink bakery boxes.

In the corner was a desk with file folders covering most of its surface. I approached it while Ryan wandered off to explore another corner.

There were several certificates and diplomas on the wall above it. I checked the names on all of them. Interesting. "I know where we are," I said.

"Where?" Ryan asked.

I picked up a beaker stamped with the words PROPERTY OF UC NIGHTSHADE and showed it to Ryan, then gestured toward the diplomas. "We're in Dr. Franken's lab. I guess now we know who's behind the appearance of the doppelgangers."

There was a click and suddenly the room was flooded with light. Dr. Franken stood in the doorway, arms folded. "That's unfortunate," she said.

She moved into the room, followed by several doppelgangers. I knew they were doppelgangers because I spotted a Mrs. Mason look-alike. Since her death had been confirmed and I hadn't heard of any zombie outbreaks, I was pretty sure I was looking at a doppelganger. I also spotted a Mort double, a Mrs. Wilder double, and even a double of our high school principal, Mr. Amadour.

I was momentarily relieved that DoppelDad wasn't among the group. Maybe the man I'd been spending so much time with wasn't a phony?

That hope was stomped to bits when he walked into the lab and took his place at Dr. Franken's side. He moved jerkily, and I realized that it must have taken a huge effort to control his movements whenever he'd been with me.

"You're the one who has been creating doppelgangers," I said to Dr. Franken. "With Mrs. Mason's help. But I don't understand why."

"I am a scientist." She sniffed. "I do not usually associate with such creatures. But the witch was necessary. I needed an exact combination of magic and science."

"For what purpose?" I said. I surveyed the group of doppelgangers. "These doppelgangers are . . ."

"Paranormal creatures, yes."

I didn't look at DoppelDad, who was standing there with about as much of an expression as a wooden puppet. I didn't want her to see how disappointed I was that he wasn't the real deal.

"We'll probably never understand exactly how you did it," Ryan said. "But I'd love to know *why*."

"Yes," I said. "It doesn't make any sense."

"Doesn't it?" Dr. Franken lifted an eyebrow.

"Most of these are copies of people of the . . ." I trailed off, not sure of how much she knew and not wanting to out any paranormal friends to a norm.

"Paranormal persuasion?" She cackled at my look of surprise.

"He tried to keep it secret, but your father's research is what clued us in to the nest of paranormals living in Nightshade."

Nest? She made them sound like some sort of vermin. I was catching on to something. The contemptuous note in her voice gave it away.

I decided to see if I could take a little dip into her mind. I hated doing that. Villains' minds were always so sludgy, so full of evil. It hurt my head to be in there too long.

"You're part of the Scourge," I accused her.

"Yes," she said. "With that witch's help," Dr. Franken continued, "I was able to replicate many involved with Nightshade's city council."

I flinched. Non-paranormals weren't supposed to know about that.

"Rose would never work for someone like you," I said. "At least not knowingly."

"True," she conceded. "But she had no idea of who I truly am. She was only interested in the science. I was careful to keep the legitimate scholarly research separate from the more creative experiments."

It was difficult to have a conversation and read a mind at the same time.

My inattention riled the good doctor and she grabbed my arm and twisted it back painfully. "Are you listening?"

"There is no need for violence," DoppelDad said.

Her head snapped around and she glared at him. "Are you challenging my authority? I say when violence is needed." She twisted my arm a little harder.

Ryan snarled and I saw that his fangs had elongated. I shook my head at him. If Dr. Franken didn't know he was a werewolf, maybe we could use it against her later.

DoppelDad responded in a soothing voice. "Of course. I am not trying to challenge your authority, but we need her cooperation, at least for a little while longer."

The doctor didn't respond, but her grip on my arm eased. That's when I slipped into her mind. I wasn't sure what I was looking for—anything that could help us.

A few minutes in there were enough to learn that the doctor was certifiably insane, which I was already clued in to. The other fact I gleaned from her left me gasping, although I tried to maintain an outward calm.

She ordered DoppelDad to tie up me and Ryan, and the doppelgangers to empty her desk of all its contents. "And hurry," she added.

"But we're hungry," one of the doubles said. He tugged on Dr. Franken's sleeve. I didn't recognize him at first because he was wearing a Members Only jacket and a loud Hawaiian-print shirt with shorts, but I was pretty sure it was a replica of the president of Nightshade's only bank.

"I don't have time to feed you now," Dr. Franken replied. "You'll have to wait."

There was a little grumbling, but the doubles went back to work. A couple of them started dragging furniture in front of the door to the lab, to barricade it.

"I don't like the look of that," I whispered to Ryan. "Dr. Franken obviously doesn't want anyone to get in."

"Or us to get out," he said.

"Make sure those knots are tight," Dr. Franken ordered as DoppelDad worked on securing our hands behind our backs.

"Yes, doctor," he answered obediently, but the binds around my wrists didn't feel especially tight.

At least DoppelDad had tied Ryan and me very close together. His arms were bound much more tightly than mine, I noticed, and he strained against the bonds.

"Why is she taking her files?" I whispered to Ryan.

"I think she may be leaving town," he replied. "She has to know that everyone is on to her. We know what's going on and as soon as we get out of here, so will the city council."

"*If* we get out of here," I said.

"What should we do?"

"I don't know, but we have to do something." I moved my hands, but the ropes wouldn't budge. Maybe I could use telekinesis after all.

I concentrated and then tried the rope again. It definitely gave when I moved. I slowly moved my wrists, careful not to attract the doctor's attention. She was focused on clearing out the lab and only glanced over once or twice.

"My hands are free," I said to Ryan. I slid my hands into my sweatshirt pockets, hoping to find my cell phone or something. Instead, my fingers found the cookies we'd bought at Slim's. What good were sweets to me at a time like this?

Plenty good, considering that we were in a room full of hungry doppelgangers.

Mort's double picked that moment to dig in his heels. "No more work," he stated. "Donuts."

The rest of the doubles crowded around her. As they loomed over Dr. Franken, I managed to reach over and untie Ryan. The doubles' mutterings were becoming ominous, when the lights flickered, then everything went dark.

CHAPTER **TWENTY-THREE**

It was completely silent in the lab for a minute. But then there was a knock on the laboratory door, and Chief Mendez's voice came through. "Dr. Franken, open up. I have a few questions for you."

I heard Dr. Franken say in a low voice, "It's locked and barricaded. That'll give us a few minutes. Through the tunnel and hurry. Giordano, you know what to do."

At first I thought she was talking to me, but then I realized that she called all the doubles by the last name of the original. She was talking to my DoppelDad.

The lab was still dark and I could only make out hazy shapes, but I heard the sounds of Dr. Franken's creations exiting. I thought they'd all gone, but then I heard the sound of something being poured and the snick of a lighter.

"You've got to be kidding me!" I said. "They're actually going to set fire to the lab. With us still in it?"

Dr. Franken said, "You always were a smart girl." I saw her

face after she lit a match. Then she threw it but didn't watch to see if it caught. She headed for the tunnel.

Time to use the powers Poppy had been coaching me on. To my relief, I managed to move the fire extinguisher across the room and get it to douse the flame before it reached the pool of what I suspected was a highly combustible chemical or plain old gasoline. From the smell, I gathered Dr. Franken had gone the traditional route: Gas.

I needed to do something, anything. Anything besides panic, that is.

Ryan and I needed to leave, but our choices were following the doctor through the tunnel or exiting the lab some other way.

Our best chance was to move the barricades from in front of the lab door. I concentrated, hard, and then finally, the heavy tables skidded across the floor. The door was still locked, but I could hear Chief Mendez giving orders.

There was a pause and then the sound of footsteps returning. Dr. Franken back to finish the job?

Instead, my DoppelDad approached me. "Daisy, I'm going to untie you and your friend. But you can't go out the tunnel with me. It's not safe. You'll have to find another way out."

I showed him my hands. "Already taken care of."

I felt a pang when he touched my face. "That's my girl."

"I'm not, though, am I?"

He looked at me a moment. "No," he replied. "But I wish you were."

I dug into my pocket and handed him the cookie. "For the road."

He took it from me with a smile. "Thank you."

"You'd better go," I said.

Just then the door burst open and Chief Mendez walked in, followed by Samantha's dad.

DoppelDad launched himself at the tunnel opening and disappeared.

"We've got to get out of here," I said. "There are chemicals everywhere and Dr. Franken poured gas all over the furniture."

We ran out of the building and retreated to a safe distance at the end of the street.

Chief Mendez was on his radio calling for fire trucks and for safety personnel to evacuate the building. The fire was out, but there were still volatile chemicals in the room.

"What about Dr. Franken and the doubles?" I asked Ryan's dad.

"I already have men stationed at the mouth of the tunnel. They'll get them when they emerge," he replied.

Sam's dad said, "Daisy, remember, he's not your father. He may look like him, but he's just a copy." I wasn't sure who he was trying to convince, me or himself.

"I know, Mr. Devereaux."

I had something to tell my family, something I'd discovered when reading Dr. Franken's mind, but I wanted to wait until my mom was home, too. Maybe the news would wipe the sad look off Poppy's face. She'd been convinced that Dad's double was the real thing, I was sure of it.

Ryan and I hitched a ride back downtown with Samantha's dad. I called my sisters on the way and gave them a rundown of what had happened. Mr. Devereaux slowed in front of the police station, where all the action seemed to be.

We parked the car and hopped out.

Poppy and Rose were already there, standing at the edge of a crowd, who were all watching the drama unfold.

"What's happening?" I said.

"They've arrested Dr. Franken for attempted murder and a bunch of other things," Poppy said. "They're taking her to the state police station."

Deputy Denton had Dr. Franken in cuffs. He put her in the squad car and drove off. But no one seemed to know what to do about the doubles. Without their leader, the doubles milled around the station parking lot, surrounded by wary-looking police. Mort's double was still whining about being hungry, and his complaints were getting louder and louder.

I noticed Mr. Devereaux avoided looking at the double of my dad. DoppelDad gave me a little wave when he saw us, but his hand was trembling. The rest of the doubles looked to be in worse shape. Some of them were holding their stomachs and groaning.

DoppelDad dashed next door to the donut shop and started rummaging through the garbage.

Ryan said, "What is he doing?"

DoppelDad was dumpster-diving again. *Eeww.* The other doppels followed suit.

"What's wrong with them?" Rose said in horror.

"They're hungry," I said. "I think they need sugar."

Ryan said, "I'll go buy a box of donuts. That should tide them over."

I smiled at him gratefully. DoppelDad was a phony, but I didn't want him to suffer.

That reminded me. I needed to tell my sisters what I'd discovered when I dipped into Dr. Franken's mind. I pulled them aside, but before I could spill it, Mort's double collapsed.

Like a row of bowling pins, the rest of the doppelgangers fell to the ground. DoppelDad was the last to fall. I rushed to his side, with Rose and Poppy swift on my heels.

I grabbed DoppelDad's hand. "Ryan will be here any minute, with donuts. Just hang on!"

"It's too late," he said. "But Daisy, I want you to know I was proud to be your dad, even though I'm not the real thing."

I choked back a sob. It was awful to see them all suffering like this. How could Dr. Franken do such a thing?

"And there's one more thing," he said. "Your father, your real one, I mean. He's—"

"Shh. Don't talk," I said. "I know, he's still alive."

"How did you know?" he wheezed.

"Dr. Franken's mind was full of information. I'm psychic, re-member?" I gave Rose a guilty look. I hadn't had a chance to tell her.

"The Scourge," he said. "Did you find out where—" His sentence ended on a gasp and he fell silent.

I looked around. The doppelgangers were all slowly melt-ing. Within minutes, most of them had disappeared completely.

Ryan came back, carrying a pink box, which he dropped as the last doppelganger, my DoppelDad, disappeared. I saw tears cascading down my sisters' cheeks.

Ryan put his arms around me. "What happened?"

"They just all evaporated." I choked back a tear.

Rose said, "There must have been a weakness in their makeup."

"They all were jonesing hard for sugar right before they died," I said. "I think Dr. Franken hadn't been feeding them properly."

"At the lab, they were all complaining that they were starv-ing," Ryan added.

Then everyone fell silent. We stayed there until the crowd left, not talking. It was late, but none of us felt like going home. No one felt like doing anything.

CHAPTER TWENTY-FOUR

Finally, Poppy said, with a falsely bright smile, "Who's hungry? It looks like Slim's is still open."

I thought food would probably choke me right now, but I played along. "I could use a coffee," I said.

Ryan kissed the top of my head. "Me, too. I'll see if Dad wants to join us when he's through."

He went to talk to his dad, and then we headed for the front door of Slim's, right across the street from the precinct. Poppy made a beeline for our favorite table.

Flo was working and she grabbed a pot of coffee and several cups and brought it over to our table. "I heard you had a rough night," she said.

"The roughest." I smiled at her gratefully. I was thankful she didn't ask any questions about what had happened. Knowing Flo, she probably already knew the entire story, anyway.

I heard a giggle and looked over. Natalie was in a corner booth, talking animatedly to what seemed to be nothing, but I knew it was Slim when I heard a deep laugh. He sounded happy.

Evidently, she'd gotten over being mad about his spying on her grandmother.

I whispered to Flo, "I guess they made up?"

"I guess they did." She sounded gleeful. "You know, Natalie's good for Slim. He's much happier since they started dating. It's not easy being . . . different."

I looked again toward the booth where they sat. "They seem good together."

"They are," she said. "But Natalie's familiar keeps leaving cat hair all over the bathroom."

"Cat hair? You mean Natalie's moved in?"

She nodded. "Still, he's happy. That's what matters."

After she'd taken our orders, I looked around the table at my friends and family. I wanted to tell all of them what I'd learned in the professor's mucky mind, but I wasn't sure how to talk to them about it.

A thought struck me. "Dr. Franken admitted she planned to replace council members with doppelgangers."

"That would mean she would have control over Nightshade's paranormal community," Poppy said.

"And she'd ruin their reputations while she did it, just for fun," Rose said indignantly.

I thought about it. "That's probably why DoppelDad was chasing all those girls. To make our real dad look bad."

"Either that or Dr. Franken planned to murder the real

council members and replace them with their doppelgangers," Ryan said grimly.

Penny Edwards walked in and I wondered why Dr. Franken had chosen to make a double of her. It was obvious to me now that the *nice* Penny had to be a fake.

It made me sad to think of it. I liked the Penny Edwards double much better than the real thing.

Poppy broached the subject that was on all our minds, and none too gently. "So what was DoppelDad talking about when he said he *knew* Dad was still alive?"

"I wanted to talk to everyone about that," I replied. I grabbed Ryan's hand for support. "When I was reading Dr. Franken's mind, it confirmed that she was part of the Scourge and they abducted Dad to use his research on paranormal genes. I only had a second, so I didn't find out anything else."

Rose said, "It's shocking to think that someone at UC Nightshade was involved with the Scourge. Dad probably trusted Dr. Franken, and she gave him up to the enemy."

There was silence around the table.

Poppy said softly, "I knew it. I knew he would never leave us. Not willingly."

"What are we going to do now?" Rose said.

"Maybe we can get her to talk," I suggested.

"Or I can make her tell us the hard way," Rose said. My normally sweet sister looked menacing.

We hadn't noticed that Chief Mendez had strolled up to our table until he cleared his throat. "I'm afraid that won't be possible," he said. "Dr. Franken fooled us. It turns out we arrested her doppelganger. By the time the deputy realized his mistake, the real doctor had escaped. We have an APB out, but so far there's no sign of her anywhere."

"She's probably long gone," Rose said. "I'll bet she's headed for the Scourge's headquarters or one of their safe houses."

Everyone around the table looked glum. Even the arrival of the food didn't cheer anyone up. Poppy halfheartedly picked at a fry.

Sean and Samantha rushed in. "We heard there was a fire at the lab," Samantha said. "Is everyone okay?"

"It's a long story," I told her. "But we're all fine."

Sean pulled up a couple of chairs and they joined us.

"Let's look on the bright side," Ryan said. "We know a lot more than we did before. We know your dad is alive, he's been held captive, and that the Scourge is involved. It's a start."

Rose smiled at him. "It certainly is."

Nicholas said, "We'll help, Daisy. Everyone will."

As Ryan had said, it was a start. I finally believed that my father hadn't deserted us. I'd wasted years doubting him, but now it was time to make up for that. We'd look for him. It would be dangerous, taking on the Scourge, but we had our friends and family in Nightshade to help us.

I slid out of the booth and put a quarter in the jukebox.

Maybe Lil had something to tell me, something that I was finally ready to hear.

"Where's my father?" I said, before punching a random selection. "I Wanna Be Sedated" by the Ramones came on and my shoulders slumped. The jukebox didn't have a clue.

I went back to the table. "Any luck?" Ryan asked.

"I don't think so," I said. But then the music cut off and a song I'd never heard came on.

"What is this?" I said.

My sisters shrugged, but Chief Mendez answered, "'Working My Way Back to You' by Frankie Valli."

Rose's cell rang. "Hi, Mom," she said, after looking at the number. "Yes, we're all here."

She listened, looking stunned. "I'll let *you* tell them. Hang on while I put you on speaker," she managed to say after a moment.

Whatever it was, it was big news. Poppy picked up on it, too. "What? What is it?"

Rose held up the phone with shaking hands. Mom's voice came through loud and clear. "Girls, I'm bringing your father home."

I think we made all the right noises, but after the phone call ended, we sat there silently, barely daring to hope. Was it possible that the *real* Rafe Giordano was finally coming home? Was this what my mother's secret mission in Italy had been all about?

I knew that, sooner or later, my father would come back to us and all my questions would be answered. After all, we were in Nightshade and Slim's jukebox had never been wrong before.

You just had to listen very closely. You had to listen with your heart.

Acknowledgments

Thanks to the fabulous people at Houghton Mifflin Harcourt, including Sarah, Barb, Jen, and Julie. Thanks to Marissa Perez and Tim Warner for great song suggestions. Thanks to Indie 103.1 for playing the best music ever. Thanks to Elise Broach, Mary Pearson, and Melissa Wyatt for letting me use their names for nefarious purposes (in the books, of course!) Thanks to LJ and Terry for putting up with my angsting. Big thanks to the best in-laws in the world. And thanks to my husband, who never lets me take myself too seriously.

Marlene Perez is the author of *Dead Is the New Black*, *Dead Is a State of Mind*, *Love in the Corner Pocket*, and *Unexpected Development*, an ALA Quick Pick for Reluctant Young Adult Readers. She lives in Orange County, California, and has a sweet tooth to rival a doppelganger's.

www.marleneperez.com

GET MORE DEAD

with these other books by Marlene Perez

Welcome to Nightshade, California—a small town full of secrets. It's home to the psychic Giordano sisters, who have a way of getting mixed up in mysteries. During their investigations, they run across everything from pom-pom-shaking vampires to shape-shifting boyfriends to a clue-spewing jukebox. With their psychic powers and some sisterly support, they can crack any case!

Is a vampire on the loose at Nightshade High? And could it be the most popular girl in school? To find out, Daisy does the unthinkable . . . she joins the cheerleading squad.

There's a gorgeous new guy in town, and he wants Daisy to be his prom date. But Daisy's already got a mysteriously moody boyfriend to deal with, and a murder to solve. Soon, the fur is flying.

Double, double, Nig...

Who would have thought the notoriously [...] could get *twice* as weird? The summer before Daisy Giordano's senior year, it does.

With their mom working on a case overseas, the Giordano sisters are on their own. These smart psychic teens have no trouble taking care of themselves. They score jobs: Daisy starts working at her favorite diner, Slim's; beach-loving Poppy mans a snack stand on the boardwalk; and Rose lands a coveted position as a research assistant to the mysterious Dr. Franken.

But then summer gets strange. Residents of Nightshade are suddenly seeing double. Doppelgangers—look-alikes of familiar friends and neighbors—are popping up all over town. Daisy, Rose, and Poppy think it's a coincidence, until the rumors start that their father, who disappeared several years ago, is back in Nightshade. Perhaps the girls won't be having a parent-free summer after all.

Meanwhile, Daisy's boyfriend, Ryan, is spending all of his time training for football, and like the other guys on the team, he's grown enormous almost overnight. Could the players be resorting to extreme measures to win?

Between psychic predictions, sugar rushes, and beach parties, the Giordano sisters get to the bottom of these mysteries and more.

www.marleneperez.com

DON'T MISS THESE OTHER BOOKS BY MARLENE PEREZ:

$7.99/H

ISBN-13: 978-0-15-206216-3

G RAPHIA

Houghton Mifflin Harcourt
www.graphiabooks.com
Cover photo © 2009 Rubber Ball